Searching
for
September

A Novel

Robin A. Lieberman

the three
tomatoes
Book Publishing

Published May 2021

ISBN: 978-1-7364949-5-0
Library of Congress Control Number: 2021908980

For information address:
The Three Tomatoes Book Publishing
6 Soundview Rd.
Glen Cove, NY 11542
Web address: www.thethreetomatoespublishing.com

Cover illustration: Samantha Rae Goodrich
Cover graphics and interior design: Susan Herbst
Author's photo: Jen Harris

*Dedicated to my children
Samantha Rae and Dean Spencer
who have validated that my commitment to parenting
has been life's greatest journey
that needs no destination.*

PROLOGUE

It is undeniably painful to reminisce about my final hours in Teddy and Lily's house. Standing in the middle of their study and being commanded to leave the premises, like a trespasser, was devastating. I was evicted from a life I had settled into. Was it Lily's worst nightmare to lose her mom and now lose me? Were her eyes fixated on her bedroom door hoping I would walk through it to tuck her in? She sleeps peacefully when she's tucked in with my melodic, "Sweet dreams, Sweet Pea," and then I dim the light and close her door halfway. Lily and I had developed a routine and now I'll never be Teddy's other half, and Lily and I will only be a memory to each other. That bastard castrated anything that was good and, like an unskilled surgeon, removed a healthy organ.

On that evening Teddy asked me to leave their house and I did, carrying my wet boots in my hands. Once outside, I sat down on the snow-covered lawn to pull them on. I have no memory of walking through the rooms of the house, upon my final exit, or taking inventory of what would no longer be familiar. I left everything behind. It would have been too traumatic to collect my clothing and memories and stuff them into one suitcase and several trash bags. Closing the empty drawers would make me feel sick to my stomach so it was easier, emotionally, to walk out knowing that my presence in their home remained through my possessions. My shoes, oh, my damn shoes; yes, I needed new shoes anyway and a fresh path to walk on.

The seat of my jeans quickly became soaked from the wet snow. When I looked back, Teddy was standing inside the garage watching me, and then a few seconds later had disappeared from view as he rolled down the garage door on another chapter of my life. I looked up at the cold gray sky and debris was falling, falling, falling. Falling from the sky with a deafening sound to remind me of how disconcerting my life has really been. Once the fragments settled onto the ground around me, a tiny stream of light peeked through the darkness and I thought about the book *Goodnight Moon*. Goodnight stars, goodnight air, goodnight noises everywhere.

All of Teddy's noise and aggressive chatter were eventually eliminated from my life, as well as Lily's sweet chirping in my ear like little girls do. Teddy robbed me of everything in a surreptitious way. Why would he lash out at me, unprovoked? I had no experience with narcissism to know that his inner wounds erupted from an unstable identity and deep feelings of worthlessness. When he verbally beat me up, I never understood that his violent episodes weren't about me. In those terrifying moments, I internalized the abuse and tried to figure out what I did wrong. Then during my recovery Teddy would turn on a dime and convince me that he was giving me God's greatest gifts, giving me all of himself with Lily included. All the while he was filling his pockets with my trust, my good intentions, my passion, and my selflessness. In the end he emp-tied his pockets into the trash, lit a match, and stoked the fire. He had me watch the best parts of myself burn. The agony of being discarded left me fragile and confused. As I stepped back from the flames, I felt like a refugee looking for a place to recover. Wide-eyed, I watched the warm, radiant flames die down to sparks, then noticed that something was left behind in the embers. It was the one thing that would save me.

Our faceless figures chase the night
Under the spell of city lights

To find another with whom to bare our souls
In search of passion to make us whole

Perspective fades when lust is found
And recklessly lifts us off the ground

To move us to an unknown space
Then swiftly leaves without a trace

Lust is the cloud that blocks our view
To hide the things we know are true
And when it passes, the dream dies, too

CHAPTER 1

1950s Me

My middle-aged expectations are strongly influenced by personal history so when I found Teddy, my needle in the haystack, I was eager to embark on our romantic journey. This is my story.

In my early twenties I entered into the sacred union of marriage with billows of white clouds dancing around my head. Our wedding day rang in a new chapter of our lives with all of the bells and whistles. I anticipated that every day that followed would be magical, budding into something extraordinary that would last for a lifetime. I waited patiently on that marital platform for the train's headlight to shine through the tunnel, waiting for the fairy tale to begin. At twenty-three years old I had not gained enough sexual and emotional experience to fully share myself with another, therefore it was difficult to grasp the reins of marriage. I operated on my "little girl dream," that magic will usher us off that platform.

As we matured I explored my feelings, both good and bad. Self-analysis became an ongoing process in my pursuit to seek depth in our relationship. While the stars were perfectly aligned with how we appeared on paper, there was something lacking. I dropped my needs by the wayside, leaving them unattended, and remained hopeful that we would grow closer. Neither of us were getting what we needed and with all of the tools in our marital toolbox, how could we repair feelings that we couldn't connect with? Heaven knows that we tried.

Magic doesn't exist and it saddened me that I could never board that train. My husband and I could not be all things to each other, but more often than not there was an echo in the canyon—a hollowness. Communication toward the end of our marital life span wasn't strong enough to overturn the emptiness, and my personal best was all I could contribute, all that I was capable of at that stage of my life.

Is there life after divorce? The naked truth is that the world has changed and it's been tough to change with it. As a divorced, middle-aged woman now seasoned with life experience, I've been on a perpetual merry-go-round to meet an honest and open-minded man with whom I have chemistry. A man who can be taken at face value and, as time passes, will have the same amount of worth as when I put my faith into him. I'm talking about "the one." This is not a pencil to the paper task, but kismet. In Yiddish it's called one's *bechert*, one's soul mate or destiny.

I've always thought about marriage, one of the most coveted unions, very idealistically. In my preteen years I recall a weekend at my grandparents' house where I stumbled upon several 1950s pamphlets that belonged to my mother.

The impetus in the 1950s was for the woman to serve the

man to keep a happy and stress-free home. Unequivocally her place was on the home front and subservience was commonplace, but not in a denigrating manner. These pamphlets branded solid ideals in my head and as I became an adult, "old-fashioned me" entered marriage still philosophizing what I had read. What had functioned decades ago can no longer be employed in this day and age, but for years I fantasized about being that 1950s woman where perfection was portrayed.

So much of our world has changed, but part of me still wants to be the woman of that era.

I've held on tightly to some of those ideals because it brings a smile to my face to imagine the comfort of simplicity. Reality smacks me on the side of the head that so much of the world is broken, but my core believes that honest relationships are the true adhesive.

As a single mother in a neighborhood with few divorced families, I became connected through Sadie's and Jack's schools and sports teams. Having been married for over a decade and divorced when the children were young, you quickly establish which friends and neighbors are the keepers. The disappearance of friends is not necessarily about my lifestyle change, but the insecurities of the unhappily married not wanting to connect with their own misery.

Several friends deserted our friendship once I was no longer part of a couple. They experienced feelings of loss when thinking about the Saturday night couples' soiree beginning with wine and cheese at the house, and now would no longer be. Their selfishness was disappointing. They never considered what it might feel like to be in my situation, on the opposite end of the stick. For many, the concept of divorce conjures thoughts of their uncertain future, thoughts they need to dismiss.

Some women who reached their forties had let themselves go and no amount of makeup could mask the sadness of an unfulfilled life. From the age of twenty-one, I maintained a serious workout routine several days a week in addition to becoming a kickboxing fanatic. With a toned body, large firm breasts, never-ending thin legs, and a fashionable but not over-the-top wardrobe, I was a looker. If I pulled on a pair of inexpensive ripped jeans with a Western belt and a T-shirt I could nail it. What man doesn't want to walk into a room and be proud of his wife? I say this without conceit. Taking care of myself was always part of a regimen, a "me" thing.

My world was unfulfilled in some respects, too, but I gave myself a good dose of beating myself up in private quarters for not understanding where I felt disconnected. In my heart of hearts there was a chasm and I wasn't able to liberate my deep feelings of despair.

We abandoned our unhappy marriage after years of an uphill battle and I relished the thought of that 1 percent chance of finding true happiness. It was worth the risk of being alone.

Eventually, I found Teddy.

CHAPTER 2

Meeting Teddy

We found each other on a frigid January evening in a trendy Manhattan restaurant. Thursday happy hour at The Headless Horseman guarantees a bustling upscale singles scene. The lofty cost of eighteen dollars for a glass of chardonnay beats going to a dive bar and sifting through men wearing hooded sweatshirts and backward baseball caps. Undeniably, I upped my game when I moved to Manhattan.

When I lived in suburbia I sought out venues that booked a good band, losing myself in the classic or Southern rock tunes that made me feel more age appropriate. The music buffered as a distraction from the playful, bullshit banter among empty-headed men and women. The female competition for a man's attention, sporting fake tits in push-up bras and delivering sexual innuendos for that complimentary cocktail, was nauseating to watch. The scene became disappointing very quickly, and I went home feeling empty.

My diversion from those singles scene hot spots was the occasional Sundance film with married girlfriends when their husbands wanted to join a neighborhood card game. The suburbs offered several upbeat French bistros with great menus, also a weekend favorite with the same married girlfriends. Graced with the opportunity to dab on some lipstick and venture out, they dusted off their designer bags for a night on the town. The problem? My thirty-year-old soul in my middle-aged body was not ready to retreat at nine o'clock. They were prepared to pack it in after the sweetness of their dessert filled their bellies and commanded that they call it a night. I was never ready to saunter back to my empty home in Finches Corners to crawl under the bedsheets alone. My children, launched, no longer lived with me. Their sweet pictures hung in dated frames and our once impressive furniture read passé. Single life becomes more complex with age and I desperately needed a change, so I sold my house and headed to New York City.

Sade's "The Color of Love" reverberates through the speakers while bodies intermingle at The Headless Horseman's crowded bar area. There's always a degree of competition for attention in a singles scene, but Manhattan clientele seem to do it in a chicer way. Strategically positioning myself close to a group of men, I'm open to and eager for conversation. Someone tries to edge past me and my purse drops off my shoulder and onto the floor. As I juggle a glass of wine and my coat to retrieve it, the man is already squatting by my knees to pick it up.

"So sorry, love, please let me get that," he says apologetically.

As he pulls himself up to a standing position his eyes lock

with mine.

"Th-thank you." I am breathless! His chiseled cheekbones and warm eyes have taken me hostage. Our one glance screams chemistry and moments like these are rare—few and far between. It's always in the eyes and, no doubt, my emerald eyes have captivated him, snagged his attention. They're one of my greatest features, a conversation piece, so everyone says.

"No problem, dear. Apologies again."

Continuing on his way, he looks back once and is gone.

Swiftly moving through the sea of bodies, my Adonis disappears into the private back room. His scent lingers and butterflies flutter around in my stomach. Holding on tightly to our evanescent connection, I'm disinterested in the cluster of men and other occurrences around me. Like a geisha girl, I shuffle in small steps through the herd of bison to drop my coat on a window seat where others have bypassed paying a coat check charge.

I'm always self-conscious going to a bar when there's no plan to meet a friend or a date. Scrolling through my phone, or sipping a cocktail, serves as a welcome diversion until I'm approached or a situation lends itself to my starting a conversation. The chardonnay tastes expensive and I take tiny sips, swirling it around in my mouth. Surely it's because of the cost per glass and is likely a J. Lohr that sells for $9.99 at Big Dad's Wines and Liquors. After nursing my cocktail for another twenty minutes I mosey to the restroom. Passing through the crowd, the private back room on the right summons me to take a peek inside.

Women are dressed business casual and the men look dapper in their dark suits. My five-foot-ten-inch stature, wearing a warm blush merino wool sweater, black skinny jeans, and a Swarovski crystal belt, would compellingly stand out and make a statement if I were to enter.

"No Adonis? Where the heck is he?" I mumble, and I'm a creep for spying on his event.

Autographed photos of famous people who have dined at The Headless Horseman line the narrow hallway leading to the restrooms. The Dames door opens to a beautifully designed ladies' room with an impressive variety of pump hand soaps and embossed disposable cloth hand towels. The LED lights reveal every wrinkle and blemish and it takes just a few minutes to touch up my lip liner and wipe away the tiny smudges underneath my eyes.

"Can I squeeze in next to you?" asks a young woman who already looks like a walking cosmetic bag, harsh and unapproachable.

"Sure, the spot is yours."

Exiting the bathroom, I catch a glimpse of the Adonis entering the Gents door, so I crouch down in a corner of the hallway and sit back on my heels. Fumbling aimlessly through my purse to stall for time, I hope to intercept Mr. Adonis when he reappears.

"Uh, uh-oh...What the...?"

A woman whisks by me, knocks me over on my ass, and my half-filled wine glass now sits next to me in large, broken pieces. I'm beyond humiliation.

"Ma'am, let me help you up," offers a waiter standing over me with an outstretched hand.

"Thank you, but I can handle this one," a strong voice chimes in. "If you take care of the spill, I'll take care of the lady."

The Adonis grabs one of my hands and uses his other to

gather my purse.

"Hello there. I'm Teddy, and you are?"

"I'm Seppie. Thank you, I'm embarrassed, but appreciate that you came to my rescue. This is quite a sight!"

"It's the least I can do after knocking into you at the bar area. You seem to be having a rough night getting bumped around," he says apologetically with a laugh. "Are you a regular here?"

"I've been here a few times, but no, not often. You?"

"My firm is having its after-Christmas party. Holiday time is a struggle for most to find an available night out. You know, commitments to family, friends, and other parties reign over anything that's work-related. We schedule this event every year, which also gives our employees a chance to introduce their significant other if they choose to have someone accompany them."

"It's fabulous that your firm plans for this. I'm sure you'd agree that we gain different perspectives on employees, and the employers for that matter, outside of the work environment. My school holds annual holiday and year-end parties and, oh boy, the personalities that emerge after a few cocktails are alarming! Well, I'm certain your guests are waiting for you to return. I'm pleased to have made your aquaint—"

"Same, thank you."

His smile and stare are killer, and I've been undressing him with my eyes, right down to his skivvies.

"If I keep you any longer from your party, I may sweep you away," I said in a coquettish voice.

"No worries. Let me replace your cocktail before I return to the Blue Room. Your poison is?"

"That's very generous. A chardonnay please, and thank

you."

Oh good Lord, put a fork in me. I'm done! It crossed my mind that he might ask me to join him at his party, assuming he's flying solo, but he ushered me back to the bar and raised his finger in the air to catch the bartender's attention for service. The bar area had become more crowded and the aromatic battle of colognes infused the air.

"Here's my business card in case you ever need an attorney." He smiled.

As Teddy reached for his wallet, I noticed he wasn't wearing a wedding band. Interestingly, when you're single it's a habit to glance at everyone's ring finger.

"Are you here with someone or...waiting for someone?" Teddy asked.

Thinking quickly, I fibbed.

"My coworker arranged to meet me, but she's running behind schedule, so I'm not sure she'll make it. I'll wait a bit longer."

Teddy raised his hand, again, for service, his eyes darting back and forth to locate the bartender. His smile turned into a scowl, and I sensed his impatience. Finally, the bartender made his way over to us.

"Yes, sir, what can I get for you?"

"What is your best chardonnay by the glass?"

He turned his back to check the selection.

"I have a 2017 French Bouchard Père et Fils," he called back. "Unfortunately, we don't offer this chardonnay by the glass."

I expected that Teddy would have ordered a happy hour drink.

"That's fine. I'll buy the bottle and you can refill the lady's glass as she wishes."

"Will do. May I have your credit card?

"Just add it to my tab. I'm Teodoro Zezza, hosting my firm's event in your Blue Room. Please take care of the lady," he stated with a smile, reached for his wallet, and removed a twenty-dollar bill.

"Thanks, pal, sure thing. Consider it done."

The twinkle in the bartender's eye lit up the room.

"Seppie. That is your name?" asked Teddy. "Unique. Is that short for another name?"

"Yes, it's short for September."

"Very nice. All right then, September, I'm excusing myself to return to my party. They'll begin to wonder if I've been kidnapped! You have my card, and it was a pleasure."

"Likewise."

I'll feel silly standing alone at the bar with a bottle of wine in a silver bucket. Teddy vanished before I could properly thank him.

"Would you like my seat?" offers the man sitting on the barstool in front of me.

"Aha, I see that chivalry is alive and well. Thank you." I positioned myself on the stool to enjoy a wine that I never would have ordered for myself. Raising the glass to my lips, the buttery texture was a prelude to the rich taste of dark cherry and licorice, capturing every taste bud before it slid down my throat. This is luxury, what I deserve!

"I'm John, by the way. An entire bottle of wine? Nice."

"Hi, John. I'm Seppie. A pleasure."

John continued to engage me in small talk and I answered his questions robotically. Surely he's picking up on my disinterest. John has a ruggedly handsome look, but his badly wrinkled button-down with a curled-up collar in desperate need of ironing is an eyesore. Negotiating my next move is weighing heavily on me, knowing I will feel uncomfortable if Teddy slithers out of the Blue Room in an hour to see me in the same spot where he left me, drinking his expensive wine. That simply cannot happen.

Glued to the barstool I pull out my phone and take a picture of Teddy's business card, my only way to connect with him if I misplace the card.

Pucchi, Pucchi, and Zezza
Attorneys at Law

In the lower right corner of the card his name, Teodoro Zezza, appears with the office and fax number. Did he give me his number as a potential client or to connect with him on a personal level?

Will Teddy return to the bar to check on me? The thought spun around in my head as the wine relaxed me. I don't want to be sitting here when his event ends. Is it unreasonable to expect that he could have asked me to join him?

The bartender, paying keen attention after pocketing a twenty-dollar tip, notices that my glass is almost empty and signals me for a refill.

"Yes, please," I mouthed, and nodded my head.

He wrapped a cloth napkin around the neck of the bottle and replenished my glass. A woman seated two stools down was served an order of lobster sliders and sweet potato fries, which would really hit the spot, but I am financially conservative when I go out. It's less expensive to prepare dinner at home, and allows me to indulge in weekly manicures and visits to high-end lounges for a happy hour cocktail. My spending is prioritized because working on a teacher's salary has its limitations.

Forty-five minutes have passed. I'm out! It's time for Cinderella to leave the ball and head home. Once I abandon my seat my night will end and that makes me feel so sad. The butterflies in my tummy won't stop dancing, but I love that feeling of trying to catch my breath. More than half a bottle of chardonnay is sitting in the bucket and incredibly wasteful to leave it.

"John, would you like the rest of this chardonnay? I must be going."

It feels good to offer it to a man whose puppy dog eyes have been vying for my attention.

"Well sure, thank you. Sorry to see you go."

"Enjoy, and have a good night."

Edging my way over to the window seat, I sift through the pile of coats and scarves and pull mine from the stack. My arms feel toasty warm sliding them into the coat sleeves. One last look toward the Blue Room with hopes of Teddy emerging turns up a negative result.

No Teddy.

The wind outside is fierce, slamming against the restaurant doors as I battle to push them open. Alas, I'm greeted with a sharp chill that stings my cheeks and I walk out into the street to hail a cab home.

CHAPTER 3

Chicks, Ducks, Geese, and Men by the Dozens

The winter chill settled in my bones, but I remain emotionally warmed by the very thought of Teddy. Many times it has crossed my mind to pull out Teddy's business card and call, but I procrastinate to avoid the disappointment of not receiving a favorable response. Quite frankly, if he had felt a connection at The Headless Horseman, he could have asked for my number. Handing me a business card made it too impersonal to reach out to him. How awkward would it be to leave a message on his office line reminding him that I'm the klutz he met during a happy hour, or leave a vague message with his secretary with hopes that he'll remember me? My indecision to take that leap of faith created a lapse in time.

For several consecutive Thursdays I visited The Headless Horseman during their happy hour with high hopes that Teddy would seek me out. I stayed for two hours and nursed one drink. No Teddy. Other evenings, I accept online dates from a cast of characters who make the "meet and greet" process disheartening and time-consuming. Primping for two hours is often not worth the five minutes it takes to know that my date is a "no go." I'll courteously saddle myself to a barstool for forty-five minutes and make small talk with a man who is unkissable and unfuckable at first sight. It never ceases to amaze me that financially successful men don't consider investing a nickel in their appearance. Their profiles establish that they are well traveled, enjoy fine dining, and own a tux, yet their yellow teeth, crooked teeth, or missing teeth don't seem to bother them. Based on my observations, it's the teeth in the back of their mouths that they don't replace and the spaces can be seen with an ear-to-ear smile. Attractive? Not!

I'll stroll into the room with my skinny legs, like a great egret, and get a once-over with a condescending comment such as, "Wow, I can work with that!" Of course you can work with this, pal. I've passed middle age and have sculpted my body for the past thirty or so years. With great passion I want to ask, "Have you ever looked inside your mouth because honestly, I can't work with that?"

Close friends have told me that my communication skills can charm a genie out of his bottle. Before I head out for a date, I inject myself with a good dose of positivity and look forward to having fun. Though a man may not match up on a variety of levels, I can find a common thread to create substantial flow of conversation. Seppie is pleasant and engaging, but men are not seeking female friendship. If there's no romantic vision, trust me, they won't waste their time or shekels. If men were seeking platonic relationships there are many whom I would enlist. In several circumstances I've asked if they would consider a friendship, but they are emphatic about "not needing another friend."

Most candidates look unsightly in comparison to their profile pictures. With slim to no redeeming physical qualities, I determined that it costs more in hair product, a few spritzes of Coco Chanel, and taxis than their generous eight-dollar happy hour drink. Meetups can become exhausting so now I schedule them close to home. I save on cab fare and sometimes return home in time to catch an episode of my favorite Showtime series, an evening that will not be a total bust.

Recently, I was getting ready for a date with a gentleman who texted me to say he arrived early to find an outside table on the street, perfect for people watching. Walking over to the restaurant I spotted him sitting in front wearing a 1980s bomber jacket—some of the leather was peeling off by the elbows when I got a closer look.

"How did you know it was me? I'm impressed," he asked with surprise when I approached the table.

I could tell the big fella was happy, and just smiled. I'm conditioned to believe that the most unattractive troll in the room must be my date. There wasn't one feature that I found remotely appealing and I was annoyed that I had to sit with this hobgoblin for an hour. When I saw the excitement on his face as if he had hit the fucking jackpot, I wanted to beat the crap out of him.

The tiny bowl of guacamole and unlimited chips were delicious and I sipped my margarita down to the melted ice cubes. After an hour and fifteen minutes passed, I politely ended the evening. Bye-bye, big fella.

I've experienced it all from the wealthy man who will overthink ordering the $10.50 bite-size fish taco appetizer to share, at dinner hour no less, to a first-time dinner date where

I'm introduced to the waitstaff as his girlfriend. It's been my experience that a man will press a little harder to get the most out of a date if he's paying for an entrée. Distinctly I remember the latter.

Bryan, an attorney living in Manhattan, called me several times during a two-week span while on his business trip. Excited as a pubescent schoolboy, he could hardly wait to return home to finally meet me. Clearly, Bryan didn't think that a "cocktail and appetizer only" meetup would be a respectable initial date because he made a dinner reservation at a high-end Spanish restaurant. On the day we planned to meet he called me.

"I envision us looking into each other's eyes when we first meet and both wanting that everlasting kiss," Bryan said with delight.

After he confirmed the time, I ended the phone call quickly, then kicked myself in the ass for not canceling. His eager beaver comment was off-putting and an asinine thing to say. Every last one of us would love to have that initial feeling when we meet someone for the first time, but who the fuck says it?

When we arrived at the restaurant and were seated at our table, he stared obnoxiously into my eyes, desperately searching for that connection of which I had none. His face appeared distorted and he looked foolish. My eyes intermittently glanced up at his, out of pity, but I was primarily focused on my mesclun with the chunk of lobster meat sprawled across the mound. I was ever so grateful that during our dinner he sniffled from a residual cold, and I pretended to be a germaphobe. Yippee, no tongue, no kiss, no nothing for you at the end of the evening.

"I have my smart car parked in front. Would you like a ride

home?" he asked, which was gentlemanly.

I graciously accepted and crawled into his itty, bitty Match-box car. He zipped across town and once we reached my building's driveway the doorman opened the little tin door to haul my ass out. Bye-bye, Bryan.

There were men who were attractive and elusive, some were out of shape and thoughtful, those who said they were separated, but not legally, and then the dimwits not wearing a wedding band but show a tan line from removing their ring. Ha, I once called a cheater out on that one! But the one thing that hurls me out of my comfort zone is frugality. I don't care if you take me to Pizza Palace, but pick up the tab. For Christ's sake, don't take me up on my offer to leave a tip that will equal the cost of my one cocktail. From time to time I offer, just to see if they'll accept. Once my date said "Absolutely not," but then followed with "You can pay the next time." Fuck off! How can a professional man with grown children do that? Jesus, shouldn't that be illegal? Grow up or fund your piggy bank before you begin dating.

On one sweltering hot day after work I had a meet and greet at a local tavern with a successful ophthalmologist. Indeed, that day was a scorcher!

"May I have an iced tea with lemon, please?" I asked our waiter.

"Just a glass of ice water for me," said Eye Guy.

Ice water? Are you fucking kidding me? What a joke!

Our waiter, the poor bastard earning close to no tip, returned with the drinks and set them down on coasters.

Eye Guy looked at me then turned to our waiter and asked, "This may sound a bit strange but can I order only a basket of fries?"

Eye Guy never asked me if I wanted to order something, that cheap, inconsiderate moron. I just shook my head and we awaited the almighty basket! Once the order arrived, Eye Guy slowly plucked each fry from the basket for the duration of our date. It was painful to watch. We chatted for over an hour, the waiter refilling his water glass several times. Eye Guy left a ten-dollar bill on an $8.80 tab, but on my way to the restroom I shoveled the kid a five-dollar bill and thanked him. Bye-bye, Eye Guy.

I also recall a meetup with Richard who, after my keen investigative work, lied about his age downward of nine years on his profile. After two or three phone conversations we surely clicked and I asked him about his age. He knew that I knew, and finally shed the truth. Richard was well above the age limit that I was comfortable with, but I decided to meet him because he intrigued me on multiple levels and his pictures were youthful. It was summertime and I was desperate to take a drive out of Manhattan. His suggestion to meet at an upscale mountain house in Upstate New York that offered a spectacular lunch and privileges to the activities on its manicured grounds was perfect! I was very familiar with this place, had lodged there in the past, and was thrilled to have the opportunity to hike some of their trails or rock scramble through their well-known labyrinth. Since he and I were traveling from opposite directions it was a fair drive for both of us, though far, and the weather was picture-perfect.

After an hour and twenty minutes I arrived in the quaint town and was pleasantly surprised that he looked exactly like his pictures—classically handsome. I must say that my attire was adorable—a short multicolored 1960s swing dress with sandals. I tossed my small nylon duffel bag with my hiking sneakers and a change of clothes into the back of his Jeep. In addition, I threw a noose into the bag should I want to hang myself if the date didn't go well. His Jeep climbed to the top of the mountain as we listened to classic rock from his playlist. I was feeling an attraction to Richard and the fifteen-minute drive up that winding road was romantic.

When we arrived at the gate the booth attendant had to check for availability to accommodate two people for lunch, either in their granary or dining room. Truthfully, I was surprised that he didn't secure a reservation earlier in the week.

"Good news," she said with a smile. "There's room to seat both of you for lunch, which is almost impossible without a reservation. The cost is sixty-five dollars plus tax per person. Would you like us to valet your car once you reach the main house?"

With hesitation, Richard said, "Did you say it's sixty-five dollars per person for lunch?"

"Yes, with privileges to enjoy our grounds and our complimentary teatime at 3:00 p.m. on the porch. Shall I take your name and send you up?"

"Lunch is that expensive?" he questioned.

I cringed in the passenger seat and wished I were a mouse small enough to crawl under it. Let me understand this, a woman drives a long distance to meet a man having had multiple, lengthy phone conversations, he decides on a location and then arrives at the altar with doubt? I'm reaching for the fucking noose! Another one bites the dust.

Incredibly disappointed, I took it upon myself to save him from further humiliation.

"Perhaps we should come back here on another day when we can arrive early morning and have an entire day to enjoy the trails. Let's head back to the town and find a little restaurant with outdoor seating."

"Are you sure?" he asked with a sigh of relief in his voice.

You penny-pinching prick. Of course, I'm sure. I'm not prepared to indulge in a lavish lunch, and with each bite anticipate your scrutinizing the check. The icing on the cake would be to order a beverage that wasn't included in the price of the lunch. I felt like Maria in *The Sound of Music* when she and the von Trapp family leave their homeland on foot over those mountains. Would the captain have told her the lunch was too pricey after their arduous trek?

"Of course, no worries," I said.

We headed back to the parking lot where we met, and he parked his Jeep next to my car. I transferred my duffel bag into the trunk of my car and we journeyed, on foot, to find a place to eat.

Settling on an outdoor café with metal chairs and an umbrella, the hostess seated us next to a family with three noisy young children and I strongly considered the noose. All of us ran close thirds, as I wasn't sure if I wanted to hang Richard, those rambunctious brats, or myself.

I ordered a mint iced tea and mesclun with vegetables, cranberries, and Gorgonzola cheese. I love those mesclun salads! The "create your own salad" for $9.95 was perfectly fine, but the fiasco at the mountain house sucked the wind out of my sails.

Richard and his ex-wife did not have children, and often the pressure of raising a family is a catalyst for divorce. He disclosed that he and his wife enjoyed travel.

"Why did you and your wife divorce after twenty-one years?" I asked during our conversation while my metal chair wobbled.

"Well, we were together for twenty-one years, but not legally married. When a couple is together for that length of time it's the same as being married."

Sure, Richard, it's the same. There's no additional cost for that Get out of Jail Free card, is there? Red flag number two. He lied about his age and marital status. Not cool.

I returned home in the early evening and composed a somewhat brutal email to Richard explaining why a relationship with me will not work.

Hello Richard,

It was a pleasure to finally meet you, and you look exactly like your pictures. Hoping you arrived home safely and enjoyed the day. I believe in honesty so I'll be completely transparent. I was taken back, at first, when you were not forthcoming about your age, but was still willing to give us a chance. It's difficult to understand, though, why you wouldn't be truthful about never having been married? I, as anyone else, deserve the opportunity to decide if I think we will be a good fit based on accurate information.

I was glad to take the long drive to see you, but to drive up to the mountain house and awkwardly sit in your passenger seat while you couldn't decide if we are worth the cost of the lunch—well put yourself in my shoes. Your plan for our day was mouthwatering, only to find myself at a dry well. My suggestion to abandon lunch and the hiking was to save both of us from further embarrassment.

Wishing both of us well in our pursuit to find the right partner.

Best,

Sep

In my estimation, I was providing Richard with valuable feedback as to why he didn't get the job. Updating his résumé and paying closer attention to social cues will take him further in the dating process, so I've done a good deed. Richard's email response was uneventful, but he mentioned that he had planned to send flowers for my birthday. Taking me to lunch on the top of that mountain and simply calling me on my birthday would have made all the difference. After I read his email, all communication ended. Bye-bye, Richard.

By far, my funniest dating story is making a plan to meet Paul in a restaurant parking lot on a Monday evening. He was enjoying his summer home in the Hamptons, but we were able to meet on a particular Monday evening when he would be driving home to pay a condolence call. Little did I know that the restaurant I suggested is always closed on Mondays. Arriving slightly before 7:30 p.m. there were no other cars in the lot. Shortly thereafter an SUV pulls in and parks next to my car. We exit our vehicles and greet each other with a hug. It was obvious that he was pleased with how I looked and I felt mutual attraction.

"Did all go well with the condolence call?" I asked.

"A condolence call?" He looked puzzled.

"Yes, you asked to meet at seven thirty because you were paying a condolence call one town over, which is why we decided to meet here," I said, very confused, as well.

"I'm sorry, but I never told you that."

"Actually, you did. Are you Paul? This is strange."

"Of course, I'm Paul. Are you Julia?"

"No, I'm not Julia. I'm September. Are you getting my name confused with another date?"

Wow, I'm so disappointed.

"I'm meeting Julia here at seven thirty and I'm guessing she is late," Paul said.

"Well, I'm meeting Paul here at seven thirty and I'm guessing that he's late, too," I laughed. "This is the craziest thing that can happen. Two couples planning to meet in the same place at the same time. Can't make this up! Quite frankly, I'm upset that you're not my date. By the way, does this dress look okay?"

"Your dress looks fabulous! Can I take your number in the event that our dates don't work out for us?"

"Absolutely, great minds think alike," I said. "So...now we wait for Paul and Julia while you take my number?"

Paul waited for Julia and I waited for Paul #2, both arriving precisely at the same time. We introduced each other, smiled uncomfortably, and then disappeared in separate cars. Neither of us enjoyed our dates and at 7:00 a.m. the next morning Paul #1 was on the other end of my phone. Both of us cleared our work calendars and spent the day together, beginning with a picnic lunch. He was even more handsome than what I remembered! Two additional dates followed during that week, and he and I were really hitting it off. Paul asked me to accompany him to a black-tie affair the following month and planned to change his RSVP to two guests. With excitement, I obliged, and began combing my wardrobe for the perfect gown.

The weekend was just around the corner and Paul mentioned dinner reservations for us at A Cut Above in the Meatpacking District. Our connection seemed to be escalating quickly, potentially turning into a serious relationship. That being said, I hadn't heard from him all day Friday and he didn't return my two phone calls. Without making alternate plans I kept my Saturday evening open, hoping he just got tied up. Ghosted.

Profiles. Typically, I stay away from profiles that read a man is "stout," or has "a few extra pounds." Predictably it's much more than a few additional pounds and in my estimation, they refuse to recognize the man in the mirror. Their pictures reflect that of a man with a bicycle pump up the old poop chute, and in real life look like they're ready to explode. No joke. I'm not a cruel person, by any stretch, just realistic that people fundamentally get bigger, not smaller. I have a vision of the type of man I'm attracted to so I stay within those confines. Athletic, toned, and average seem to work best for me. There are certain characteristics or profile details that trump others when I'm searching for candidates. For example, an educated man with a profession, worldly and well traveled, will upstage my typical six feet or taller height requirement. I'll cave on the height for the profession. The teeth are still the number one asset and that has become my hard line. Encouraging people to fix their teeth equates to encouraging them to manage their emotional issues. It's an exercise in futility.

Online dating profile pictures, to a large degree, have become a form of entertainment when boredom sets in. Honestly, what are these men thinking? Holding a large northern pike that was just dredged from the ocean? Not sexy, swipe left.

Selfie pictures that are taken in a bathroom mirror with moldy plastic shower curtains behind them yield "no sleepovers there." Swipe left.

If the selfie is taken in a public bathroom I may have the good fortune to see a urinal in the background. Seriously, when would I ever have an opportunity to see a urinal? Swipe left.

I get a charge out of the photo showing four men sitting around a birthday cake, the Bumble candidate and his grown sons. "Check please, I'll swipe right if I can meet the son on the right."

In a particular photo a man looked exactly like Stanley Tucci, the serial killer in the movie, *The Lovely Bones.* In good conscience, I never could have a meetup with this man, though nice-looking. I'd spend my hour on the barstool imagining myself prancing through the cornfields while being persuaded to check out his underground murder chamber. Yep, swipe left again.

The funniest is the picture where the man is sitting next to a person who has been clipped from the photo. However, the arm is still around his shoulder and she's wearing a wedding ring. Nice! Swipe left.

The profile summaries that say the following are a swift swipe left:

"Hello and thanks for stopping by." (Golly, jeepers.)

"Wishing everyone the best of luck!" (That sounds like a goddamn sinking ship.)

"Let's meet for a drink, dinner afterward if there's chemistry." (So, at seven o'clock on a Saturday night should I eat a few crackers with cheese prior to the date, or dress like a whore to ensure I won't starve?)

"I like fine dinning." (Dinning? Really?)

"I'm five foot five, but I have a tall personality." (Put on your elevator shoes and have less personality, please.)

"Looking for someone drama free." (It isn't fun if there's no drama!)

"I'm great in the bedroom and have the tools to match!"

(Check please! I like that, but please curb your enthusiasm.)

"Graduated from The School of Hard Knocks." (What does that even mean, a dumbass?)

Though humorous, it takes a short time to burn out from dating. When you meet a man like Teddy and experience the nicely packaged charm and the chemistry, wrapped up with a bow, there's little to no comparison.

I progressed through the dating game like a trouper, but it was difficult to get Teddy's image out of my head. If, on any of these dates, a man wanted to hold my hand it was uncomfortable. There's a deep intimacy attached to holding a person's hand and it stems from my teenage years. If a boy were to hold my hand it meant that he was my boyfriend, a very serious thing. Strangely, holding my hand feels much more intimate than a kiss. Chemistry has to hit me immediately because I can't "grow into someone." It's either there, or it's not. The intensity that I felt with Teddy is something I have not experienced with anyone else. Given the countless number of men whom I've met, not one sent a shiver down my spine.

Frustrated, I decided to get in touch with Teddy.

CHAPTER 4

Reconnecting with Teddy

"Good afternoon, Pucchi, Pucchi, and Zezza. This is Francesca speaking—how may I direct your call?"

"Yes, hello. I'd like to be connected to Teodoro Zezza, please."

"I believe he's just out of a meeting. Who can I say is calling?"

"September Webb," I responded with a detectable quiver in my voice.

"Thank you, and this is regarding?"

Jesus, lady, you're killing me here. Uh...this is regarding the gazelle that fell on her ass at The Headless Horseman and is trying to hunt down the hot-looking attorney who bought her a drink.

"This is a personal call."

"One moment, please."

"Hello?" came a deep voice from the other end of the phone.

"Hi, Teddy?"

"Hello, September, how are you? If I recall you prefer a nickname? Sep, Septem,Sep..."

"Yes, Seppie. Some time has passed and I hoped you'd remember me. Is this a good time to talk?"

"It isn't. I'm swamped with work, but will be glad to reach out to you when I'm free. I'll transfer you back to Francesca and ask her to take down your number."

"Sure, sorry to interrupt your work. I'll look forward to your call."

"Very well, then. Talk soon."

I waited for the transfer to go through to his receptionist, but heard a click and then a dial tone to follow.

Fuck, fuck, fuckity, fuck! Is he kidding me? Let's talk about the definition of stranded! With my heart pounding out of my chest, I waited a few moments and immediately called back the number.

"Good afternoon, Pucchi, Pucchi, and Zezza. This is Francesca speaking—how may I direct your call?"

"Yes, good afternoon. This is September Webb. Mr. Zezza and I spoke briefly and he tried to transfer me back to you so I can leave him my number."

"Of course," Francesca replied politely, "I'm ready to take your number.

After reciting my number, I asked her to repeat it to be sure she recorded it correctly.

"Thank you so much, Francesca. Have a wonderful day."

Every hour that passed felt like I was sitting on death row. Tethered to my phone, it was impossible to focus on anything but Teddy's return phone call. If a store didn't have adequate reception, I'd walk out. When I washed my hair the shower door was slightly open, the phone propped up on the floor just outside. I was as nervous as a long-tailed cat in a room filled with rocking chairs! Sheer lunacy.

I was incredibly distracted during my workday, checking for text messages and missed calls every five minutes because my phone needed to be on vibrate. Sitting in meetings was torturous, knowing I couldn't stand up and walk out at any moment. From time to time the group leaders would enforce the drop box policy for cell phones to deter from the constant phone checking by all participants. That drop box left me dead in the water!

The hours passed, and then days, with no word from Teddy. I blamed myself for waiting too long to reach out to him. Surely, my number is sitting on his desk among a few others with zero sense of urgency. For all I know it was swept aside and sandwiched between the pages of a legal pad, only to be found months from now with no memory of who Seppie is. Moving forward, I will block any thoughts about Teddy.

It is the middle of March and spring is around the corner. A March day when I can leave the apartment with a sweater and pack away the heavy winter coat. Tonight I have a blind date, which is rare. My neighbor knocked on my door last week and mentioned that her husband's coworker was looking to meet someone outside of the dating website circuit.

"Daniel is a lovely man," said Pamela. "My husband has worked with him for years. He recently posted his profile on one of the sites, but he would rather meet a woman through a friend or acquaintance. Look, you never know. Can I give him your number?"

"Of course, I would be delighted to meet him. Thank your husband, and I'll let you know if Daniel reaches out to me."

It will be refreshing to meet a man who hasn't been pecked by the vultures. When a newbie develops an online dating profile the piranhas smell the meat in the water and attack their prey. There's no better way to describe it.

Tonight will be my first date after taking a hiatus; I needed a mental break. Daniel has chosen a jazz club for cocktails and light bites, and arranged to pick me up in front of my apartment building. It's a polite gesture and I'm certain he isn't an ax murderer because it's a setup. Normally I would meet at the venue. I began getting ready for my date two hours ahead of time, sipping a glass of wine in the process. It relaxes me. I've chosen a black skirt with a camisole and a short jean jacket. Opaque tights and suede heels make the outfit look sexy and dressy and perfect for a jazz club.

At seven fifteen the concierge buzzes my intercom.

"Good evening, Ms. Webb. I have Daniel here?"

"Thank you, be right down."

Tossing a small tin of mints into my cross-body bag, I grab my jacket and take one last look in the mirror. I feel good about myself and, as always, have a smile on my face.

The elevator door opens on the lobby floor and I catch a nod of approval from the concierge and smile back.

"Good evening, Ms. Webb. Daniel is outside," he says, as he opens the lobby door.

Daniel is waiting by the passenger door.

"You must be Daniel?"

"I am, and you look great! Ready to go?"

"Yes, indeed," I state, as I gave him a hug.

"Let me help you into the car."

Immediately I can tell he's happy that I am his date. During our drive we shared personal trivia while occasionally glancing over at each other.

"Thank you for joining me tonight at Strings."

"You're quite welcome, Daniel. The last time I went to a jazz club was in New Orleans several years ago."

"Well, it's my favorite jazz club, among many, and one of Manhattan's best-kept secrets. I know you'll enjoy it and want to go back."

As we approached Strings, surprisingly he found street parking just around the corner. In Manhattan, I call this "good parking karma." He was mannerly in every way, paying close attention to detail such as opening doors and walking on the curbside of the street.

When we arrived at Strings the line stretched around the corner.

"Follow me, September."

Daniel put his arm around my shoulder and steered me toward the front of the line. He shook the gentleman's hand at the door and we were directed down a dark, narrow staircase. Once inside the jazz club the maître d' seated us front and center, removed the Reserved sign, and lit the small candle. Daniel was either mafia or just a very good patron! I'm reminded of Karen on her first date with Henry Hill in *Goodfellas*. The only difference is that Daniel didn't grease ten people's hands with cash on the way in. No doubt Daniel planned ahead, and I appreciate that.

"Can I start us off with a nice cab or do you prefer something other than cabernet?" Daniel asked.

"A cab would be great. I drink both red and white. Thank you."

Daniel motioned the waitress to our table and placed the order. Our evening was off to a successful start. For sure I would accept a second date from him, although instinctively I wasn't drawn to him sexually. He is pleasant and well put together. His adult children are launched, making him completely available for a serious relationship.

An hour or so into the evening, enjoying the music, wine, and charcuterie, my phone started vibrating in my purse. To be respectful I always keep my phone in my purse because it's a distraction. If my complete attention is not focused on the person I'm with, in any situation, it would be plain rude. Sliding the top zipper across my bag I peek in and it's a call coming in from Teddy's office number, a number I have memorized.

"Daniel, I'm so sorry. My son is calling me. I'll need to step out for just a minute," I whispered impulsively.

By the time I jumped out of my seat and frantically scurried to the entrance it became a missed call with no voice message that followed. If he's calling on the office number he must be working late.

Damn it, Seppie, good job! You missed his call! Teddy, why couldn't you have called me when I was alone!

My teeth are clenched so tightly they could crumble.

Scattered thoughts about Teddy have me in a tailspin. I've waited for his call for weeks, and now he calls when I'm chained to Daniel for the evening! Absurdly I'm feeling angry with Daniel, a true gentleman, for being with me tonight when all I want to do is hail a cab to my apartment and call Teddy. I don't want to be here and have my opportunity to speak with Teddy stifled.

What to do, what to do?

I pressed down on Call Back, and a voice answered on the third ring.

"Hello, this is Teodoro Zezza."

"Yes, hello Teddy, this is September, September Webb. How have you been?"

The inflection rising in my voice is certainly coming through as nervous excitement.

"Hello September, I'm sorry I didn't return your call sooner, but there was no message other than your name and number. Maybe your call to me was placed in error," he explained apologetically. "How can I help you?"

"Oh boy," I said, "this is awkward. You and I met more than two months ago at The Headless Horseman when you were hosting your firm's annual holiday party. We bumped into each other and I spilled my wine? It was a while ago so you may not remember."

"Indeed, I remember. Yes. A short while after I was helping you up from the floor outside the restroom area, but I'm not accusing you of having too much to drink, dear."

"Definitely not from consuming too much alcohol," I giggled. "I had kneeled down to take something out of my—"

"Whoa, time-out. It's quite all right. I am not the sobriety police nor am I judging you. And I do remember that night. Your beautiful eyes, specifically," he said, charming the pants off me.

Naughty me would allow him to do that.

There was awkward silence and I looked back into the club to see if Daniel was coming to find me. I was enjoying my conversation and desperately wanted to find a quiet place to sit down.

"It sounds like you're out somewhere with the noise in the background," Teddy probed.

"Actually yes, I'm out for dinner with my son."

"Well, I won't keep you. If you're free one night I'd like to take you for dinner."

"I would really love that, Teddy. What does your schedule look like?" I asked, trying to pin something down.

"The weekends tend to be easier for me. I'm a widower with a young daughter and during the week my time is spent with Lily. I can sneak away on a Saturday evening when Lily can stay with her sitter. Would that work for you?"

"It absolutely would," I replied. "If I'm not sounding too forward, I'm free next weekend if—"

"There you are, September," called Daniel. "You're missing the show. Is everything okay?"

I covered the phone with my hand as Daniel walked toward me.

"Yes," I said nervously. "I'll be back inside in a moment.I'm so sorry."

Daniel turned and walked back to the table, thank God, but I felt like an ogre.

"Apologies, Teddy, my son just walked outside to tell me that our dinner has been brought to the table. I am free next weekend if you'd like to see me and I promise, you won't be picking me up from the floor."

"Very well, September. I'll be in touch. Have a good night."

"You, as well."

The call ended.

I inhaled deeply and slowly released the air, taking a cleansing breath before joining Daniel back at our table.

It's difficult to remember the nuances of the remainder of my evening with Daniel. The music sounded as though it was playing so far away, but we were seated up front. We consumed the entire bottle of Stags' Leap, but I don't recall tasting the bouquet in that fine cab. I have no memory of the drive back to my apartment, and when Daniel said goodbye with a gentle, nonaggressive kiss, my lips were numb. I felt nothing. My mind was playing tricks on me, concomitantly feeling euphoria and despair.

"You're a beautiful woman, September. I'd like to take you out again. I'm sorry that your son had a difficult breakup with his girlfriend, but it sounds like your conversation calmed him down. Such a good mom."

I gave Daniel an appreciative hug, our torsos inches apart.

"Thank you, thank you, Daniel for introducing me to Strings. We'll talk soon."

Colton opened the lobby door and I disappeared into the building.

Bye-bye, Daniel.

CHAPTER 5

The Carriage Comes for Cinderella

Teddy followed up with a phone call the following day, leaving a voice message with the best time to reach him. I had scheduled myself for a kickboxing class at noon, then ran a few errands until the magical hour of three o'clock. Propped up on my sofa, I was relieved to be in a quiet place with no distractions to chat. On a small pad of paper I jotted down notes in two separate columns. In one column I listed things that I want to share about myself, and in the other column, questions I could ask Teddy, but nothing too intrusive.

Not wanting to appear desperate, I waited until 3:10 to return Teddy's call. In a monotone voice, he answered on the second ring.

"Hello, September. How is your day?"

"Very good, Teddy, but please call me Seppie."

"Oh yes. Apologies. Seppie," he said agreeably.

"I exercised today and accomplished a few tasks, but now

I'm settled in and happy to hear your voice."

"Thank you, that's kind of you to say. And dinner with your son last night?"

I had to switch gears and remember that I had been on a date with Daniel. After ghosting a few of Daniel's texts, a phone call is in order to let him know that we're not a good fit.

"Yes, thank you for asking. Dinner with Jack is always special."

My Jewish guilt gnaws at me when I'm not being truthful.

"If you're still available for a Saturday night date I'll make arrangements for us to meet in the city. I live in Greenwich, Connecticut, but glad to come your way. How does eight o'clock sound?"

"Eight o'clock is perfect. Just let me know when you decide on a place."

"Great, Seppie. It sounds like we have a plan. Have a good week and I'll look forward to seeing you again."

"Same here," I said, folding the paper in half. "Until soon."

Our phone call ended.

I'll pull out all the stops in preparation for our date. A visit to my colorist and the nail salon, for sure, but the biggest decision is what to wear and that will depend upon the venue. An eight o'clock meetup could mean cocktails only, since he'll likely have dinner with Lily.

A text rolls in from Teddy on Wednesday that we'll be going to Spice, a restaurant on Great Barron Street on the Lower East Side, a gentrified area. We didn't communicate again prior to our date and when I Googled the restaurant, nothing surfaced. There isn't a website for Spice and friends who know the city well have never heard of it. It would be nice to take a peek at the menu, should Teddy offer dinner, and also get a sense of the restaurant's attire. Dead end!

Saturday crept up quickly and most of the day was spent decompressing from the workweek. This seems too good to be true. Teddy is too good to be true. For weeks I've been memorializing a man I barely know. Tonight will be perfect. I will be perfect!

At five o'clock I began getting ready for the date and shot Teddy a text for the restaurant's address. Calling for an Uber pool at seven fifteen should give me enough time. The fare is reduced in an Uber pool and often there are no additional riders.

My place is a mess! Clothes are strewn all over the apartment from changing up shoes, skirts, dresses...you name it. It's difficult to find my level of perfection each time I pass by the full-length mirror, but at 6:20 I reckoned with wearing a tight leather skirt and a black angora halter. The grand winner! My four-inch suede Stuart Weitzman's put me over the top, both in height and on the attractiveness meter.

Twang, pling, pling. The sound of harps light up my phone at six forty-five with a call coming in from Teddy and I'm hesitant to answer. Please don't cancel, please don't!

"Hello, Teddy," I answered, just above a whisper.

"Good evening, Seppie. Are you looking forward to our evening?" His voice is deep and controlled.

"Very much so. I plan to leave my apartment at seven thirty, but did not find an address for Spice."

"I'll be picking you up. What is your address? I'm leaving the house shortly and would never expect you to meet me somewhere." The astonishment in his voice is loud and clear.

"Oh, I had no idea that..." I stumbled on my words.

"Seppie," he said firmly, "I'm not sure what your experience has been with other men, but a lady should presume that her date is picking her up and escorting her out for the evening. Never expect less for yourself. I should reach your address at 7:30ish and will be driving a black Carrera. Text me your address, please."

"Very well, I'll send it to you now."

"Great, see you soon." He ended the call.

I should have thought more of myself than to jump into public transportation, but I just didn't know. My experience with most of the other men has been to meet somewhere, and that occurs because you haven't met the person or it's someone you don't know well.

The hardwood floors are taking a beating from my pacing back and forth, making frequent visits to the bathroom mirror and touching up another area of my face each time. Nervousness has consumed me with the overwhelming thought that Teddy doesn't believe I value myself. Sinking my body into the sofa, I try to employ some deep breathing.

"In and out, in and out. Close your eyes, Seppie, and think about the wonderful hours ahead."

Buzz.

At 7:40 I'm roused from my quiet anticipation by the intercom.

"Thank you, Colton. I'm on my way down."

One last glance in the mirror, and then I'm out the door.

The elevator seemed to take an inordinate amount of time to reach my floor, but my adrenaline started to flow when I heard it roar a few floors below. The thought of finally seeing Teddy is enchanting. He's absolutely right; I should expect the world from a man!

When the doors opened on the lobby floor Teddy was

standing with Colton.

"I was just telling Colton that this building has the most beautiful woman living here."

Teddy's arms are extended for a hug.

"Well, thank you. I'm so glad my two special men have met," I said, as I moved in closer to hug Teddy.

Colton, one of several doormen in my building, takes very good care of me and it goes a long way to acknowledge him, not only for providing a service.

Teddy's presence is strong and he looks impressive wearing a dark navy blazer over a gray cashmere V-neck sweater and gray slacks. His scent is Terre d'Hermès, a fragrance I know well.

"Have a safe trip home, Colton, if I don't see you later," I said endearingly.

I noticed the exchange of cash from Teddy's hand to Colton's.

"Will do, Ms. Webb, and enjoy your evening."

Colton escorted us outside and opened Teddy's passenger door for me.

The black Porsche Carrera with luggage interior is intimidating, but I am composed and won't comment on the car. Teddy slithered into the driver's seat and pulled the car up to the end of the circular driveway, stopped, and shifted the car into Park. His arm stretched to the back seat and returned with a small turquoise box from Tiffany & Co.

"Something special to begin the evening as a thank you for joining me," he said with soft charm. "Please accept my gift. Tonight you are my lady."

For a woman who doesn't shut her mouth, I was speechless.

"I don't know what to say," I said, trying to catch my breath, "this is too...too generous."

"There's no need to say anything, love. Please. Open it."

Slowly I untied the white satin ribbon and removed the cover from the bottom of the box. What could he have chosen since he doesn't know anything about me? I removed the turquoise pouch, and inside it found a beautiful pearl and sterling bracelet, something I would expect for a birthday gift. No man has ever lavished me with a gift on a first date, no less from Tiffany.

"Teddy, this is stunning. I—"

"Allow me," he interrupted, as he twisted his body in the bucket seat.

Teddy's hands are well maintained, his fingernails buffed with no extraneous cuticles. I watched him fasten it on my wrist.

With my head tilted down watching him find the clasp, I raised only my eyes to look at him and he caught my glance.

"Keep your eyes where they are and don't move, Seppie," he commanded in a slow, sensual tone. "Stay in the moment."

I didn't move or breathe. My breath had already left me the evening we met at The Headless Horseman.

Once he secured the bracelet on my wrist, he looked up and our eyes reengaged. I am lost in him, a man I barely know, and my emotions are running rampant. He leaned across the console that divided our celestial bodies and held my chin in the palm of his hand. Oh, how I want to be reckless and impulsive, and not a lady. My fierce energy is spiraling from the frustration of longing for him. His mouth approached mine, but he didn't allow our lips to touch. I could feel his breath on me.

"Shall we begin our evening's adventure?" he murmured as

he released my chin.

"Aren't you going to kiss me?" I said coyly.

"No."

The Porsche, like a big black spider, prowled the city streets, and the bracelet captured the light from the streetlamps. When we reached a red light, Teddy lifted my hand from my lap, kissed the top of it, and brought it onto his lap.

Still holding my breath, I closed my eyes. This is my magic carpet ride.

We reached our destination and the Porsche crawled into an outdoor lot with a Lot Full sign at its entrance. The attendant opened my door to assist me and I grabbed his hand tightly to pull myself out from the seat of the sports car. These sport cars sit very low to the ground.

"Thank you, Johan. We should return in about an hour and a half," Teddy informed him as he handed him the key and a twenty-dollar bill.

"No need to worry, Mr. Z, it's all good here."

Teddy, walking slightly ahead of me, stretches his arm back and I take hold of his hand. He ushers me down Great Barron Street and my eyes remain peeled for Spice, but don't see a sign. After walking past a dimly lit bodega and a hole-in-the-wall Mexican restaurant called Gracias Padre, we turn into a small store that has their shelves stocked with spices. The store, warm and fragrant, carries every variety of spice imaginable from around the globe. Some are contained in jars and some in cellophane bags. Barrels of loose spices line one of the walls.

A man appears from behind the counter to greet Teddy and me.

"Good evening, Mr. Zezza. Welcome back! And who is your

lovely friend?"

"Thank you, Daichi. It's a pleasure to be back. This is September and it's her first time dining here. Is our table ready for us?"

"Welcome, September. We are glad to have you with us tonight."

Daichi, a thin, frail-looking man whose clothing hung limply around his body frame, had us follow him. Teddy brushed his hand with money.

The bamboo wood panel to the left of the cash register holds colorful leaflets describing the origin and uses for the spices. Daichi pulls down on a small lever on the adjacent wall, allowing the panel to open. A young woman appears on the other side.

"This is my daughter, Kanya. She will escort you to your table. May I check your coats?"

"Yes, of course," Teddy said, and assisted me with my coat before removing his own.

"Welcome. Please follow me," Kanya said in a barely audible voice.

Teddy and I stepped into a spectacular hidden gem! Lamps with multicolored bulbs and turquoise velvet chairs hugging small tables constructed an unparalleled ambiance. Beaded curtains surrounding each table create privacy and inspire intimacy. Our reserved table is tucked away in an alcove, and this family-owned jewel accommodates only eight tables. No website was found because the clientele is strictly from word of mouth.

Teddy and I were seated and immediately served Thai mango martinis, their specialty cocktail.

"There is no standard menu. I have some favorites, though,

that I think you'll enjoy. May I order for us?" Teddy asked with confidence. "Anything that you're allergic to or simply do not eat?"

"Thank you, I prefer that you do. I just don't eat raw."

My fairy tale continued to unfold inside our beaded cocoon, and I kept touching the Tiffany bracelet as reassurance that it didn't fall off my wrist. We were brought papaya and duck salad, glass noodle vegetable soup, and a beef satay appetizer for starters. Our main courses were seafood pad thai and lime fish with pineapple fried rice. Halfway through my third martini I was feeling way too good and uninhibited. The numbness at the tip of my nose is a signal that I'm reaching my limit of alcohol consumption.

"Teddy, have you wondered what it might be like to kiss me? Oopsies. Apologies. Am I being forward?" I asked with a girlish giggle.

"Actually, Seppie, I haven't. Why? Have you wondered about me?"

"Liar, liar, pants on fire. I think that you have. And yes, I imagine your kiss to be very warm and welcoming."

There's no doubt that I'm acting a little puerile, while spilling out my thoughts.

Teddy pulled himself up from his chair and crept over to my side of the table.

"Look at me, Seppie," he commanded, as he lowered himself to my face level. He pressed his lips against mine and held them there without parting them. My entire body tingles and I wanted to curl up in a corner with him for the rest of the night.

That arrogant bastard, I detest him for not giving in to me.

His lips remained gently pressed against mine with his eyes piercing through my soul. Gently, I grab the back of his hair while teasingly biting his bottom lip. He refuses to part his lips and is still waiting me out on the kiss. Tugging on his hair with more force, he opens his mouth. His tongue is warm and sweet as he rolls it around in my mouth. Playing a little cat and mouse game, I latch on to it, sucking it tenderly with my lips and tongue. It's everything I imagined it would be. Teddy is everything I could hope for.

Teddy repositioned himself back in his chair. The slight swaying and glistening of the beaded curtains has me hypnotized while Teddy plays with the bracelet on my wrist. *Teddy, I want to tell you that I'm falling in love. Am I in love with you, or with the thought of being in love? Oh, it's just semantics.* The alcohol, combined with flashbacks of all my shitty dates, is playing tricks on me. Please sweep me away, far away.

"Can I bring you some dessert? It's on the house, as always," offered our waiter.

Teddy looked toward me.

"Thank you, I am so full, and enjoyed every dish that was served," I answered respectfully.

"Seppie, would you like to bring some dessert home? Their Thai gelatin with shredded coconut topping is heavenly and you can enjoy it tomorrow." Teddy sounds so convincing.

"Really, I'm good. I'm really good."

"Very well, then. I'll have to bring this lady here for another date. Just the check, please."

Once the check was paid, I took my cue from Teddy that it was time to leave.

Feeling tipsy, I managed to stand up from the table and walk to the door like a lady. Kanya unlatched the secret door and we walked through it, leading us back into the spice store.

"A special goody bag for the lady, and I hope you will return again soon," Daichi said graciously, handing me a miniature brown shopping bag with raffia tied at the top. "A sampling of spices with instructions."

"Thank you, Daichi. It was a pleasure to meet you. This was a magical dining experience."

He handed us our coats and Teddy buttoned me up like a parent would a child. That Lily is one lucky little girl to have the best daddy in the world!

With Teddy's arm tightly around my shoulder, we left Spice and strolled through the streets. When we reached the parking lot the Porsche was already running and warmed up. Johan opened the passenger door and helped me in.

The Porsche roared onto the street and I couldn't take my eyes off Teddy. After the car crawled down several blocks, I gently removed his right hand from the steering wheel and placed it in my lap, cupping it in both my hands. I don't want to go home and I don't want Teddy to drive back to Connecticut.

"I don't want you to leave," I said to Teddy in a low and muffled voice. He glanced over with a look that melted my soul. It dawned on me that my place wasn't tidy. In my frenetic state of getting ready I left my apartment looking like a department store dressing room during a post holiday clearance. It doesn't matter anyway because Teddy will be going home to Lily.

The motion of the car lulled me into a dream and when I opened my eyes we were a block from my apartment.

We pulled into the driveway and Colton, still on duty, extended his arm to help me out of the car. Teddy stepped out of the car, as well.

"Colton, would you mind babysitting my car in the circle?

I'm going to take Seppie upstairs. I'd prefer to give you a hundred dollars than to garage it."

"Not a problem, sir. I'm working a double and the eleven-to-seven shift is quiet overnight."

This is really happening.

Teddy and I rode the elevator and I fantasized about how wonderful it would be to come home to him at the close of each day. We walked arm in arm to my apartment as I blindly fumbled for my key in the bottom of my purse.

"Aha, a good find!"

"Allow me," Teddy suggested, and scooped the key out of my hand.

After several attempts to unlock the door, it finally swung open and I no longer wanted to be in control of any decisions moving forward. The alcohol continued to cloud my thinking, but warm my thoughts, while my poorly heated apartment kept a chill in my bones.

"Come here, Seppie. I'll help you off with your coat before I leave. Would you like that?"

"Would *you* like that, Teodoro?" I teased in an Italian accent, and began walking backward into my bedroom, hoping he would follow me.

He removed his coat as he crossed the threshold.

"Let's get that coat off you," he commanded, tossing his coat onto the chaise.

"Make me," I fussed, backing away from him.

"You don't really want me to chase you, Seppie, do you?"

I took baby steps toward him and, when face-to-face, placed my hands on the top of his shoulders.

"Now, that's much, much better, Seppie." He started to unfasten each button on my coat, his eyes glued to mine.

He doesn't blink once and his overconfidence is daunting, and sexy, and cocky, and...I'm on fire. Fuck you, Mr. Over-confident, thinking that you know me so well. Fuck you, Mr. Adonis, or whatever you call yourself. You're simply a prick. My eyes momentarily look away and I know that he knows I'm smitten. Damn you, Teddy Zezza!

He slides the coat off my shoulders and when he turns to place it on top of his, I position myself on the edge of the bed and lean back on my elbows.

"This is a setup, isn't it?" he asks in a very serious tone as he follows me. "Lie back and I'll finish undressing you."

Obeying his authority, I fully recline on the bed.

"Such an obedient girl."

He's pulling on the bottom of my boots as I wiggle my feet out of them. Closing my eyes, I feel Teddy's hands navigate underneath my skirt and ascend my right thigh. Oh God, I imagine him pushing himself deep inside me and the thought is intolerable. With precision, his fingers roll down each thigh high as my body tingles under his masterful technique. He's taking his time and watching my expression, watching me squirm, deliberately torturing me.

"You think you're a clever man, Teddy Zezza? It's all about you, isn't it? You arrogant—"

"Stand up, Seppie."

Propping myself back up on my elbows and spreading my legs wide, I watch him remove his shoes and socks while giving him a preview. His pants drop to the floor and he steps out of them.

"Come to me." He holds his arms out to pull me off the bed.

Still tipsy, I take hold of his hands and he lifts me off the bed like a rag doll, bringing me close to his body.

"Look at me, Seppie." His hand lifts my chin.

Pressing his lips flush against mine he unzips the side of my skirt and it falls off my hips. Strong hands cup my buttocks and his gentle caress is a mere appetizer to what will be served. Hugging each other tightly, his cashmere and my angora create their own marriage while our lips continue to press tightly against each other's. The heat of his breath seeps through the spaces between his teeth and he's ripping my heart out.

When Teddy's hands creep up the back of my halter, I follow suit and move mine underneath his sweater. Effortlessly we lift our sweaters off each other's bodies, baring our skin. Skin to skin. His chest hair, soft and intoxicating, will be my pillow tonight. Desperation pours from my eyes and he has opened the floodgates. I'm evaporating into an unknown place. Our mouths are everywhere they shouldn't be, which puts both of us right where we should be.

Straddling me on top of the featherbed my hands grab the brass bar on the headboard and dreamily I gaze out of my high-rise window. And like a metronome, a flickering blue light from a nearby tower is keeping in rhythm with our bodies' thrusts. Stripping each other of our dignity, like feral adolescents, we reached that pinnacle together. Our consensual debauchery into the wee hours of the morning imposed havoc on all of my senses until exhaustion consumed the both of us. I stayed warm underneath Teddy, while his car sat idle in the driveway.

As abruptly as the sun rose so did Teddy, to return to his daughter.

The coolness in the apartment cleared my head.

CHAPTER 6

Obsession

Teddy tells me that the sun rises and sets in my eyes, and lavishes me with an insane amount of attention. Our nightly phone calls that begin at eight o'clock last for an obscene number of hours and I jockey between two apartment phones when their batteries dwindle to a low charge. On occasion, both phones need charging and I reach for my cell. When I suggest a more abbreviated "talk time," so I can accomplish a few chores, it results in his application of guilt.

"If I, a busy attorney, prioritize spending time on the phone with you at night, are you telling me that you can't reciprocate? Remember, I also have a young daughter here."

I love talking to Teddy, but after a full day of work fielding phone calls, responding to boatloads of emails, and sitting in meetings, I'm on sensory overload by the time I arrive home. Teddy takes a break during dinnertime to spend time with Lily, but I question why more of his downtime isn't spent with her, especially surrounding her bedtime.

Teddy does have a point, though. Living alone gives me more flexibility than him, so I stay bound to the phone on speaker mode while grappling with my laundry basket as I make my way to the basement.

There are multiple phone calls in the evening and our conversation lingers past midnight. Most nights I fall asleep with the phone on my pillow. His immediate callback, the ring waking me, keeps me chatting again until two to three hours prior to my alarm clock sounding off. It must be love because no man who I had ever known wanted to chat on the phone for more than a few minutes.

Some of our conversation becomes contentious, partly due to the fact that he will expand on a topic to keep us talking, almost to the point of senselessness.

"You're divorced, Seppie. Do you love me more than your ex?"

There's no right answer to give him. If I say I will always love the father of my children, then he will criticize me for not trying to work out my marriage. If I tell Teddy that I love him more, I'm criticized for marrying a man that I didn't deeply love. When the phone call finally ends, I feel like I'm a disappointment.

I had sold my house in Finches Corners several months before meeting Teddy. The location of my new residence in Manhattan serves as a mecca for every possible want and need. An overabundance of the unimaginable! The best restaurants, cultural events, and museums can be explored within a short radius. How unlikely that I'd meet a man from the suburbs among Manhattan's finest?

Teddy, a prominent attorney and partner in a boutique

medical malpractice firm, has one young daughter to spend his time with after work; I have become his focus, too. He finds solace in my voice and daily communication, though excessive. I want to be his special woman. My cherished circle of friends has intimated that his behavior sounds obsessive and perhaps he needs an unhealthy amount of attention. It's understandable why they might be jealous.

A neighborhood grandma, Nonna Martha, is a staple in their home and paid handsomely to take care of Lily and the household chores. She has her own bedroom in Teddy's house and often stays over when he works late nights, but typically leaves after the dinner dishes are put away. If she enters his home office while he and I are on a call, I can hear his impatient tone usher her away like an intruder. These timeless conversations may appear obsessive, but I'll err on the side of true love.

Slipping unnoticeably out of a committed pre work exercise routine, I realize that the term *gym rat* can no longer describe me. It has taken tremendous loyalty to wake at 4:25 a.m. and arrive at the health club by five o'clock sharp. I, with the other exhausted early morning risers, will stand like bulls waiting to charge through the gates. Most days, now, I can barely function at work. The two or three hours of sleep each night catches up with me by noontime, and driving home has become risky.

We chat with each other, from our cars, to and from work. Our communication continues throughout the day with texts and I'm baffled how he can complete any work. I respond to his texts when I can, but will not place my job in jeopardy. On occasion I'll tell him that I'm staying late for a meeting, but arrive home my usual time to give myself the luxury of making other personal calls and catching up on life.

Teddy drives into the city where our time is uninterrupted.

"It feels good to leave Connecticut and come out of 'daddy mode' for a change," he says.

One oppressively hot August afternoon, he and I walked through a small park on the West Side and wandered into a secluded area, far from the cheering at a children's baseball game. I was wearing a pale pink cotton top with a matching skirt, and when Teddy patted my butt he could feel that I wasn't wearing panties. As much as I enjoy provoking him, I was a hound in heat in his presence. I remember that afternoon well.

Stepping around a few lost baseballs and the occasional empty water bottle, a clearing in the expanse of grass invited us to lie down and act upon our impulses. Steam rose from the ground and our clothing was drenched from the mixture of sweat and sunshine. He gently kissed me on my lips and after teasing hesitation I took his tongue into my mouth. We remained enveloped in the moment and fixated on each other's eyes, breathing life into each other. His hold on my hands was firm, pinning them to a position of constraint. I welcomed his advances and then contested them, but as my body began to relax I lost my inclination to resist. Still holding his tongue in my mouth, I felt his body upon mine. Aroused by his strength, I felt his hard passion against me, his need to release his energy, and his wanting to ride me like a mighty steed. With his hands still firmly holding mine, he detached his mouth and inched his way to my body. A chill ran through me like a freight train. I squirmed as he feverishly nudged the two large buttons on my blouse with the deftness of his mouth. My firm, round breasts peeked through with great invitation as he anticipated taking them into his custody.

I surrendered and encouraged him to begin the journey, as our hearts pounded loudly. In what seemed like seconds, he moved rhythmically inside me. Spellbound and on the threshold of bringing our swell waves to their crest, droplets of sweat from his forehead moistened my lips as the waves turned over and over. My mouth opened as I eagerly stretched for that last bead of sweat to gratify my thirst. Teddy communicated to my entire body, my breathing rising and falling, until my body elevated and my breath was taken from me. Teddy's expression revealed that he had lost his breath, too. With our bodies still entwined, our breathing slowed in harmony and we lay fulfilled. He whispered in my ear that I carry my sensuality like no other woman, and I yearned for Teddy to stay in that moment before we composed ourselves.

These sexual escapades have become the core of our relationship, and when those passionate moments end there is nothing substantial to replace them. His behavior has become unpredictable. No continuum of positive emotion or constructive dialogue bridges each episode. His random kind hearted words are quickly replaced with uncontrollable and unrelated outbursts. It must be me who, unknowingly, spurs this upheaval, but I cannot figure out how or why?

I'm grateful for the experience that generates a strong sexual charge for both of us, but after that moment is gone it is fantasy that binds me to a relationship that may gradually erode my sense of self. Teddy carries a tragedy that weighs him down, but I sustain myself in our relationship with great hope that I can bring him fulfillment. I am a true giver. My insecurity always gets the best of me and echoes that I am not entitled to more. Now that I've found great passion with someone who is wounded, I feel pigeonholed to make us work. In doing so, I risk losing my perspective and the strength to walk away. The woman who everyone views much differently than I view myself may get lost; a woman of substance easily lured into the shadows.

As far back as junior high school I wanted to be connected to a special someone and longed to be the girl who was given a heart-shaped box of chocolates on Valentine's Day. In high school, I gawked at the girls who walked around with the humongous box with their shit-eating grins. Do other women feel as incomplete as I feel? It's overwhelming to conjure up childhood emotions that still have the capacity to breathe life into my adulthood. I've abandoned the thought of finding my wings. Teddy provides so much physical passion, and I believe that all relationship gardens need tending, so I will remain with him until all moving parts stop moving. This bird isn't ready to fly.

CHAPTER 7

Monster

When he was good, he was very, very good, but when he was bad he was ugly.

After knowing Teddy for a short amount of time, he encouraged me to move in with him and Lily. Teddy and I are so taken with one another and it is a sheer delight to close my day with the security of knowing we belong to each other. This is an enormous commitment, however as a mother and seasoned educator I am confident that I can swiftly weather the storms of the challenges. I pinch myself daily because my happiness is so overwhelming that it doesn't seem real, and it's difficult to fathom the prodigious life I am now living.

A challenging task, indeed, that requires great sensitivity when I slowly make adjustments in their home that resonate "I'm here," while being respectful of the memories that made the house their home. A relationship with a widower is very different from having a relationship with a divorced man.

With Lily living in the home I pay close attention to everyone's needs, at times sacrificing my own. It's important to me, intrinsically because of who I am as a person and a mother, that should Lily's mother peek down from the heavens she would feel gratuitous to witness her child being loved and valued in her absence.

In bits and pieces, I learn about Tessa, Teddy's late wife. He speaks of her with supreme regard and places her so high on a pedestal that I could never, in my mind, come close to being the woman who he describes. Their Italian heritage was a natural bond and they fit perfectly, like a hand in glove. Like Teddy, Tessa was fluent in their native language and he said her soft voice sounded as sexy and alluring as her exterior beauty. In a twisted sort of way I believe I am special because he chose me to fill her shoes, albeit there are no similarities in our backgrounds, physical appearance, and domestication. I'm a good Jewish girl, attractive in my own right, who learned to prepare a meal when I married in my twenties. It's intimidating to know that Tessa was born into a lineage of culinary artists and mastered the art of cooking from assisting in her parents' upscale Venetian restaurant. I struggle with making a good matzo ball soup, which Teddy loves. Occasionally I'll sneak over to my mom's house to pick up a pot of hers when she's given ample notice. I avoid Teddy's kitchen like a plague, allowing him to cook and requisitioning myself to the cleanup.

As some time has passed, I no longer tiptoe past Lily's bedroom to access the master bedroom. Often, I leave our bedroom door open so she can freely enter the room to ask me a question, borrow my sweater from Daddy's closet, show me her homework, or watch me curl my hair. All the things that my daughter experienced at Lily's age and all the things little girls should. A six-year-old losing her mommy needs the guidance of a strong and loving female to assist with all of the things that a woman is trained to do.

Lily and I have become two peas in a pod, but not after a tough two years of earning her trust and helping her to feel secure with my presence. It's paramount that the people in Teddy and Lily's circle recognize that I'm here for Lily, as much as for her father. Regardless of my daughter Sadie's age, which is almost fourteen years Lily's senior, my sensitivities always precede my actions to be certain that my Sadie knows her place with me. Children at every age need comfort and reassurance.

Recently, Lily noticed that the screen saver on my phone is a photo of Sadie posing with her large funky sunglasses.

In a pouty tone Lily asked, "Hey, where's my picture?"

Lovingly, I allowed her to make a collage picture with her and Sadie so the two girls could appear on the screen. Stepping into another woman's life is an enormous challenge, but the luxury of having alone time with Lily reassures her that she can gravitate toward me as the other adult in her home. Tucking her in at night, making her special school lunches, organizing her bedroom, and eventually taking her for eyebrow waxes and manicures has become routine.

At the appropriate age to consider contact lenses she and I decided we would ask her father. Her fitting for the lenses took several weeks to schedule, mainly because it was my idea but he channeled it through "She's too young." Lily was an adorable little girl who needed a woman's touch. Lily and I had to glide around certain topics with her father because as she and I grew closer, Teddy became more controlling. His dominance never surfaced in the moment, in a conversation or situation, but his pure malice would rear its ugly head during random disagreements at random times. During those demonic episodes I was blindsided and left defenseless, and they were often in front of Lily or within her earshot.

"Lily doesn't need a mother, and you have your own children. You've had your chance to do whatever you wanted when your children were young," would be a notorious outburst from Teddy.

Lily would be left feeling confused and sad, and not wanting to discredit her father all I could do was follow her into her bedroom and tell her that I love her. The residual feelings after these surges wounded us, and it baffled me how an apology from him was never in order. Lily became so comfortable with me that at one point she became demanding. I gently, but firmly, addressed her tone with me and then proceeded to iron her special blouse for school the next day. My decision to move in with them came with careful consideration, as I would never flippantly assume accountability with anyone's child as an experiment.

So why do I stay?

I recall my teenage years, never being asked to be someone's girlfriend and with Teddy, I am the chosen one. My insecurities as a young girl still surface in my adult life, especially my need to please others. I try, with great determination, to fulfill this image of who I think Teddy wants me to be. In tender moments, Teddy tells me that I am his savior—that he never met anyone like me since Tessa's death. In one breath he'll tell me that I am his angel who fell from the sky and my world feels blissful. Then, in one of his classic uncontrollable vengeful moments, he will verbally tear down the loss of my marriage, calling me a "ring collector" and state with conviction that he will never marry me. My blissful world is crushed!

He and Tessa were happily married for many years until she passed, and Teddy had a way of making me feel as though my marriage wasn't meaningful because "until death do us part" wasn't fulfilled. It was tough to navigate his psyche and grasp what may have created his unsettling and disturbing behavior. Had Tessa's death put him over the edge? Occasionally when he consumed a substantial amount of alcohol, I was able to massage our conversation and impel him to talk about Tessa's illness, which he shared was a sudden onset, terminal, and lingered longer than what those closest to her could endure. Prior to her illness, was he verbally aggressive with Tessa? Did the beautiful and talented Princess Tessa stand up to his insolent outbursts? Was Tessa "special" simply because she was the mother of his child?

I'd welcome the opportunity to ask those questions to those closest to him, but the conversation must lend itself to the right place and time and segue from another conversation. It's difficult to imagine that these outbursts haven't surfaced in his professional relationships or friendships, but he is at a good comfort level with me and that could be the reason why I'm the recipient of his unstable behavior.

The days evolved into weeks, and then months, vacationing together and settling into a domestic atmosphere. As the mother of my own adult children, I strategically manage to give everyone my time with no one feeling abandoned. Lily and I surreptitiously discussed puberty, menstruation, rushed to the stores to select bras, and practiced the art of shaving with a real razor. I was cautious to not cross Teddy's boundaries, leaving Lily with the continued freedom of decision and Teddy to rubber-stamp everything. As his Lily became a young woman, I tried to understand Teddy's loss of control and remain sensitive to a father with a maturing daughter. However, it frustrates me that I've been invited to absorb this life and my experience as a mother and an educator isn't always valued. I sweep these maddening thoughts under the carpet and pass it off as two adults working through major life changes. This life that I richly enjoyed on so many levels, despite the tribulations, has become a microcosm of what I view as crafting a perfect future. Moving in with a widower is a serious business and we are well on our way to being solidified as a couple, and as a nuclear family.

I'm still haunted by the lonely wall hook above our bed where a wedding portrait of Tessa, sitting in a horse drawn carriage, once hung. My one caveat before moving into their home was that I would not sleep under Tessa's picture, yet since it has come down nothing has replaced it. The shelves in the bathroom that hold my toiletries were once occupied by Tessa's cosmetics and Eternity perfume, which I carefully placed under the sink's cabinet. Eternity. The name sends shivers down my spine because her sweet life never reached a fraction of that. Tessa's ravishing body deteriorated from a disease that shut down her systems. So interesting that the subtleties granting me entrance into another woman's life and home consumes me with guilt, because I love Teddy with every fiber of my being and wish that I could have had all of those "firsts" with him. Buying our first home, hosting our first Thanksgiving, and seeing Mrs. September Zezza on my mail are fantasy thoughts. My periodic jealousy remains compartmentalized, as I remind myself of where Tessa is now.

I would come to know that Tessa is more at peace six feet under than married to Teddy.

CHAPTER 8

The Photograph

Late summer I scheduled a photo shoot with the talented Robert Wheeler, highly recommended for boudoir photography. For years I considered being photographed in a sheer bodystocking with a sexy, but classy look. Everything must be perfect. A few indoor tanning sessions to even out my skin color will maintain an after-summer glow. Call it a midlife crisis, but I'm not getting younger, though I look better now than when I was in my thirties. Three decades of exercise have toned my body and I can stand nude in front of the hallway mirror and say, "Yeah, girl, you've got it!"

This photograph will be a present to me, a bucket list item getting fulfilled. I have never been in a relationship with a man who deserved to receive this kind of framed picture from me. Second thought, this would be a perfect Valentine's Day gift for Teddy, the man who has everything.

There is familiarity driving down this tree-lined street. The branches are sparse as the chill of late October changes the season. I'm deep in thought searching for 333 Shelton Avenue. Shelton Avenue is a thirteen mile stretch of a two-way, four-lane road that passes through a few unforgettable towns in Rockland County, New York. The diversity of the towns runs the gamut from dilapidated and seedy to towns that are occupied by Hasidic Jews. Though I am Jewish, my Jeep enters this very religious area that feels cold and uncongenial. I am a stranger in a strange land, an intruder to those more devout whose customs are disparate from my own. Unwelcoming as this neighborhood may seem, being surrounded by a community of people who are reclusive and serene brings a feeling of safety.

The modest two-family homes are interwoven with small window-front businesses that hang wooden shingles, some faded and weather-beaten with lettering that can barely be deciphered. 339, 341...I somehow missed the address. The next corner is a one-way street, and just past that is a small barren lot enclosed by a metal fence. Green plastic slats fit nicely into the diagonal openings of the fence and the slats that are missing allow for a bird's-eye view of the discarded rubbish beyond it. Another three blocks down I turn my Jeep around in a tar-paved lot of a corner convenience store and make my way back to find the address. Squinting to read the numbers from across the street, while watching the cars in front of me, I notice that a significantly larger home has an impressive mailbox that reads 315 Shelton Avenue. Moderately frustrated, I turn around at the next corner and my car crawls along the side of the street. With my hazards flashing I see 325, 327, 329, all private homes. 331/333 are numbered on a double mailbox by the driveway of another small house with an enormous picture glass window and chipped painted lettering that reads Tax Returns Prepared. Quickly, I flip on the directional signal and proceed down the long narrow opening designated as a driveway.

The driveway belongs to that house and another set farther back, not noticeable from the main road. The little house in the back has a wooden sign on the ground next to the door that reads 333. The driveway curves slightly at the end and opens to a grassy area that can accommodate two cars side by side. Patches of burned-out grass have divots of dry dirt and small rocks throughout the area. The neglected detached garage looks like storage for unused items that will never get disposed of. With no other car in the driveway, I sit for a few moments listening to the lull of my car engine. I duck my head slightly to look up at the ramshackle house. The screens are sad and torn and I wonder how a successful photographer's home doesn't have a suitable appearance for his craft. I'll reserve judgment and assume that the inside shows differently than the outside. How can the well-known Robert Wheeler capture a beautiful pose in a shabby room?

Intending to have no distractions I shut down my cell and store it in the glove compartment. The phone, for me like so many others, has become an addiction. With every beep, ding, and vibration my world would come to an end if it weren't answered. Mr. Wheeler's fee is charged by the hour and not by the session, so my time in the studio must be efficient taking into account a wardrobe change.

The car engine cries a low sputtering sound when I turn off the ignition. Stepping out of the driver's side I open the back door to reach for my small carry-on luggage, compartmentalized and holding everything in place including a curling iron, hair dryer, brushes, and makeup.

The onset of colder weather has captured autumn and stepping through the dirty, dried-out leaves feels depressing. As I approach the antique wooden door, I see a torn wicker basket sitting off to the side holding a soiled rag and a random wheel from a skate, stroller, or some other moveable object. There is nothing welcoming about this visit, thus far, but it's not my nature to cancel an appointment at the eleventh hour. I pull back the screen and firmly knock. No answer. After adequate wait time I knock with more force and the door jars open.

"Hello? Hello, Mr. Wheeler? Hello, are you here? It's Seppie. Seppie Webb. I have a two o'clock photo shoot." I call out with only my head through the door.

Stepping into his kitchen, dated but neat, a thin floor mat invites me to wipe my feet. No doubt it's ready for disposal with no foam padding remaining on the bottom. The mat moves around with my feet, but respectfully I give it the old college try. The Formica kitchen counter is a mossy green and looks original. Next to the sink is a light blue plastic drying rack with one bowl sitting on it. Two pieces of silverware stick up from the plastic holder, which I can imagine is grimy on the bottom, a disgusting thought! It's that one kitchen item that no one bothers to clean, like a butter dish. On the other end of the counter a wooden stand holds four-mismatched coffee mugs and it reminds me of the decor in my parents' 1960s kitchen. There's a refrigerator, stove, and toaster oven, but no microwave or dishwasher. The small square kitchen table has a plastic tablecloth with a woodsy pattern and three chairs are tucked neatly under the table. I'm curiously observant and yes, I am one of those who enjoy peeking into people's medicine cabinets and behind their shower curtains.

With uneasiness I call out again, "Mr. Wheeler? It's Seppie Webb and I'm here for the two o'clock photo shoot. Are you here? Hello?"

A deep voice returns with, "Yes, just come down the stairs by the kitchen table. I'm setting up for our appointment."

"Sure, I'll be right down."

Turning back to lock the entrance door there are three chain locks mounted in various places, but one lock seems like it would be sufficient. Remaining optimistic, I shuffle back to the staircase. The basement door is left open and gives way to a very long staircase. From the top, the staircase is lit by one exposed light bulb with a frayed hanging cord. The smell of musk incense is sweet.

"That's it, love," Mr. Wheeler calls out. "Come on down the stairs."

"Com-coming."

With my carry-on I clumsily make my way down the first few steps and the staircase appears darker at the bottom.

Stupid, stupid, girl! the voice in my head is screaming. *Your cell phone is in your car and your car is buried in the back of a hidden driveway. What are you doing? Get out of there!*

Frantically, I climb up the steps backward banging my belongings into the side of the staircase wall. Mr. Wheeler calls my name again, but I am watching the bottom of the stairwell until I reach the top step.

"Home free, home free," I say under my breath as I scurry to the back door to twist the lock open.

The fresh air greets me with a sense of freedom and I rush to my car, leaving his back door open. As I toss the carry-on into the back seat, I see Mr. Wheeler appear at his back door and as quickly as he begins his approach toward my car is as quickly as I slide into the driver's seat and lock the car.

Shabbily dressed with sharply defined facial features, there's something about his persona that haunts me, and my body stiffens. This has happened to me twice before when I've glanced at a stranger and his image triggered a feeling of discomfort with no rhyme or reason. With Mr. Wheeler now standing in front of my car I carefully back up, swing around him, and make my way down the secluded driveway. In the rearview mirror, I see him standing with his hands on his hips and I feel guilty about leaving abruptly. He likely is professional and safe and I'm worrying about nothing.

I won't turn back.

CHAPTER 9

Valentine's Day

Valentine's Day rolls around four months later and Teddy knows that Valentine's Day has always held certain magic for me. From the time that Sadie and Jack were young I acknowledged them on Valentine's Day with a sentimental card and a gift. They would wake up the morning of, and a special surprise would greet them at the kitchen table while I prepared breakfast. Now that they're adults I mail them a card and enclose a gift card to a coffee shop or other store they visit to keep the tradition.

Silly me. I'm disappointed about the photograph and realize that it would have been the perfect gift. Truth be told, there would not have been an appropriate place to display it, not at home for Lily to see and not at work on an office desk. Gift baskets are my specialty so a large red one is filled with treats for both Teddy and Lily. Something for everyone!

Every item is individually wrapped with their names to exercise discretion. Lily will open an assortment of socks, pant-ies, and headbands all in colors of red, pink, and white. She will also unwrap a large chocolate bear holding a red heart and a bag of individually wrapped chocolates to share with her friends at school.

Teddy will unwrap a sexy red thong and a provocative sheer T-shirt that I will wear to bed, but the tag on his gift says Open Privately. Included in the basket is a ninety-five-dollar bottle of Piper-Heidsieck for Teddy and a bottle of French pink lemonade for Lily. The plastic champagne glasses that I've included will invite all of us to make a toast.

Nothing is too good for Teddy and I try to incorporate "firsts" as often as I can. It makes for a better union to add experiences that haven't been part of other relationships. It could mean dining in a new restaurant or vacationing in a place that's off the beaten path. A good amount of emotion-al energy is expended on keeping our relationship strong and forthright with an element of mystique. I also believe that anything worth doing is worth doing well and I made a commitment to live in their home. No stone is left unturned. Though it would be delightful, at this stage of my life, to focus only on Teddy, there is a young girl who needs to take comfort in knowing that her world won't change with the division of her father's attention.

The morning of Valentine's Day I padded lightly down the stairs when everyone was asleep and left the beautifully wrapped basket on the kitchen counter next to the coffeepot. Both Teddy and Lily were excited to start their day with a surprise and I derive great pleasure in bringing life into their home.

As Lily unwrapped each gift she ran over to Teddy.

"Look, Daddy, oh, look what Seppie got me!"

She laid out her panties, socks, and headbands on the chair.

"Oh, Seppie, can we organize my drawers tonight?"

"You know we can, Sweet Pea."

I gave her a kiss on her forehead and wished her a Happy Valentine's Day.

"Don't forget to take the chocolates to school and share them at your lunch table," I reminded her.

"Oh, Seppie, do I have to? I want to keep them," she pouted.

"They are yours to do what you wish, but I was thinking today is the perfect day to spread the love."

Lily reluctantly put the bag of chocolates in her book bag, and I chuckled.

I love when Valentine's Day falls out on a workday! It's comical to watch staff members stroll through the lobby to pick up their flowers, delivered in a variety of ways. Most are sent in small vases with a combination of roses and other less expensive flowers added in, and throughout the day their owners proudly escort them to their classrooms. I am focused on stopping at a gourmet restaurant on the way home to pick up an expertly prepared dinner. By the time I'll reach home Teddy and Lily will be hungry and I want to make this a special surprise.

Teddy hadn't mentioned reservations for dinner so I called ahead to Chez Margaux, a French bistro, and ordered from their prix fixe menu for pickup. They're offering a four-course dinner of acorn squash ravioli, boneless lamb ribs, a tricolor salad, and choice of a chocolate or coconut cream pie for dessert. For Lily's dinner, they allowed me to substitute the lamb ribs with a farm-roasted half chicken, her favorite.

The end of the day could not come soon enough. Waking

up at five in the morning, working forty-five minutes past my normal time, and bucking traffic during my long commute home will be exhausting. I made my way to the main office to sign out and a few of the cellophane-covered vases were lined up on the counter awaiting acknowledgment. Among the vases, a long white box with a pink ribbon and a heart-shaped box of Godiva chocolates secured under the large bow stood out like an eyesore.

"Night all," I called out to the secretaries and turned to leave for the day.

"Seppie, are you really leaving without your flowers?"

Turning back, I approached the vases and began reading the gift cards.

"It's the large box!" Chrissy shouted.

Excited, surprised, and a little embarrassed because I don't want to give the impression that I'm entitled, I walk over to the box and the three people in the office pressure me to open it. How can I say no? In my two decades of working here, a box of long-stemmed roses has never been delivered on Valentine's Day, or any other day for that matter.

I lay my bags down and carry the white box over to the table. There's a card attached to the box.

Thank you for being an angel that fell from the sky
All my love, Teddy

Carefully, I untie the pink ribbon and feel tension with everyone huddled around me. Removing the box of chocolates, I invite everyone to share one with me and they gratefully oblige. The top of the long white box lifted easily and there are a dozen long-stemmed white roses beautifully separated by paper with water-filled holders on the bottom of the stems. I'm speechless. I've never received flowers in a box, though I always dreamed of them. A few "ohs and ahs" came from the secretarial choir as I secured the top of the box with the ribbon, then sheepishly said goodbye.

Holy fuck! Teddy knows how to show up and make a statement!

Pulling into the crowded parking lot behind Chez Margaux, after an arduous drive home, I rushed into the crowded bistro and charged my credit card $148. I made a litany of phone calls to family and friends, on my way back to the house, to share the news of the flowers. I'd promised to text everyone a picture of the flowers in the box before transferring them into a vase. The entire time that I had been on the phone, I didn't realize there were several missed calls from Teddy. When I tried to return his call, it went to voicemail.

In the home stretch! I'm about half a mile from the house. At each red light I impatiently watch for it to change, hitting my hand on the steering wheel as if it took longer than expected. As I turned the corner and made my way up our block, Teddy's SUV began pulling out of the driveway.

Honk, honk.

He notices my car and pulls back in, leaving room for me to park beside him.

Excited, I jump out of my car and walk over to the driver's side window. His window lowers and Teddy has an emotionless look on his face. Lily is in the passenger seat.

"Seppie, Daddy has been trying to call you," Lily shrieks. "He is taking us to a fancy-schmancy restaurant for dinner. Look, I'm wearing the red velvet dress."

"Oh my. I had no idea that you had planned something. I

worked a little bit later and then was overwhelmed by the box of roses. Teddy, I love you so much! Thank you for making Valentine's Day so very special for me. And Lily, did you surprise your friends with the chocolates?"

"Everyone loved them, even my teacher! There was enough to go around and my teacher said to say thank you for being so thoughtful," Lily boasted.

"If you're coming to dinner, then please get in the car," Teddy said in an impatient tone. "I've been trying to call you and now we're ready to leave. I want to take my girls to The Old Mill Inn and they don't take reservations. There will be a wait, I'm sure, but I have my mind set on seafood bouillabaisse. I had no idea why you weren't home and why you didn't call me, so I left you a note."

Apologetically stumbling over my words, I tried to explain.

"Well, I stopped on the way to pick up a gourmet dinner for all of us. It's from that expensive French bistro and they wrapped everything to go. The food is expertly prepared, the way you like it, and wanted to surprise you and Lily."

"Oh," Lily said, "Daddy really wants his favorite dish and he said that I could order sweet potato fries. You can share them with me."

"I picked out a roasted half chicken for my girl and lamb ribs for Daddy," I said in what I thought was a convincing tone. "The food is ready to eat now. We just need to set the table."

"If you're coming with us, then please get into the back seat," Teddy said sternly. "We want to leave and we've waited long enough."

"What am I supposed to do with all of this delicious food that I bought?" I asked with disappointment. "It was expensive and a shame to waste."

"With you, Sep, it's always about money. You can stay here and eat it or you can come with us. I won't eat food that is a day old so you can always take it for lunch tomorrow. The dog also likes lamb and we can cut some into his dish when we return home."

Upset and angry, I negotiate my next step while Teddy adjusts his rearview mirror. $148 is what I am thinking. The food will sit in my car and the receipt for $148 sits in my wallet. The flowers will remain as is because the stems are in water. Slowly I walk to my car, lock it, and crawl into the back seat of Teddy's SUV.

Happy Valentine's Day.

CHAPTER 10

The Big Day

Two years have passed since Teddy and I met at The Headless Horseman, and tonight he's hosting his firm's annual holiday party there. Last year a blizzard canceled the event. He decided on a Saturday evening, this year, and booked a room for us at the Beaumont Hotel to make it a romantic weekend. It isn't often that he leaves Lily overnight, but I encouraged him to allow her a sleepover at her best friend's house. His list of rules is extensive, but there's no doubt they will be followed.

Earlier in the day I drove to my hair salon in Finches Corners, with Lily in tow. She watched in awe as my hair was transformed into a beautiful updo with soft tendrils framing my face.

"I guess you did an amazing job, Jules, because Lily seems to like it."

"Oh, you bet I do!" yelled Lily.

"Jules, do you have time to get Lily's hair washed and styled just like mine?"

"Oh, no way! Really? No way! Really?" asked Lily excitedly.

"Way," I said. "Let's be twins!"

Lily had no idea that I made the appointment for both of us.

"I'm getting an updo, I'm getting an updo, la, la, la, la, la!" Lily sang as she twirled around in the chair.

An hour and fifteen minutes later Jules put the final touches on Lily's hair with a finishing spray and a tiny rhinestone clip on the top of her head. Lily spun around slowly in the chair, with delight, admiring her new hairstyle from every angle. Somehow, I knew this would ease her pang of not being with Daddy and me tonight.

When we left the salon, Lily and I visited Madeleine's Nails and Spa. Side by side, we chatted away like besties while I was getting my French manicure and Lily was getting a powder blue polish with silver sparkles. I've come to know Lily well and she was daydreaming about being Daddy's date this evening. It's important to make her feel special in every way knowing that she'll feel envy not being invited out with us. If Lily starts to fuss while Teddy and I are dressing up for the Blue Room it will take a lot of coaxing to settle her down, despite her sleeping at her friend's house.

Tonight will be flawless and my grand entrance into the Blue Room will be spectacular! The dress I bought was well thought out, classy, and sophisticated, but sexy in its own right. I chose a winter white A-line dress with a short matching jacket. My shoes are crème suede with a small rhinestone bow at the back of the ankle. On an educator's salary the dress and the shoes were pricey, but well worth Teddy's reaction and the reaction of those who will see me enter the Blue Room on his arm.

Several weeks ago, Teddy and I were shopping in Manhattan and he pulled me into Saks to buy me a gold leather clutch with a gold rope chain, just because. He'll be pleased to see that the clutch accessorizes perfectly with my dress. Teddy will have the most beautiful woman escorting him to his party and I will surely make him proud. One of my greatest thrills will be to bypass the bar area at The Headless Horseman when walking to the entrance of the Blue Room. I've played this scenario over and over again in my head. Teddy will take my coat, hand it off to the coat check, and then we'll enter the Blue Room as a couple. Finally, I'll be introduced to his partners and staff.

After an entire day of running around, Lily and I return to my car for the long ride home. Overtired and excited, Lily keeps the passenger's mirror hanging down so she can continue to admire herself. Out of the corner of my eye I see her reach for my ruby color lip gloss in the cup holder and she catches me watching her.

"Ah, now I'm Princess Lily! Are you mad, Seppie?" Lily asked, gazing at me with a guilty look after she dabbed a little on her finger and applied it to her lips.

"Of course I'm not mad."

It's absolutely precious to watch her alternate between making funny faces and serious faces with her mouth. When she finally closed the mirror, the sunshine hit her eyes and she slept during the remainder of the ride.

At precisely the time that we're turning off our exit, Lily awakens. Busting at the seams she can hardly wait to see her daddy.

"Wait until Daddy sees how beautiful we look," says Lily. "Hurry, hurry and park the car!"

I pull into the driveway and before the ignition is turned off Lily bolts from the car and heads to the garage door's key panel. I trail behind her.

"Seppie, you go first!" she demands. "Please, I want you to go in the house first and then introduce me as Princess Lily."

She's tugging so tightly on my jacket that I can barely walk. We enter through the garage and then through the fireproof door leading to the kitchen and see Teddy standing by the kitchen sink. The biggest smile lights up his face when he sees me and is obviously pleased with my hair. I'm warmed to the core.

In an official voice I announce, "It is my utmost pleasure to introduce to you the one, the only, Princess Lily!"

Shyly and slowly Lily steps out from behind me and stands in front of her father. Teddy looks down and his smile is replaced with a look of disappointment. Suddenly our worlds darken.

"Get upstairs and take your hair down," he said firmly. "You look like a damn twenty-year-old. And wipe that crap off your lips!"

I'm speechless! Lily storms out of the room, loudly marching up the stairs of their colonial home.

"Puttana, cazzo puttana," Teddy says under his breath. Once we hear her bedroom door slam, I am summoned to the den.

"I'm sorry, Teddy, but I'm going up to Lily's room with her," I say with conviction.

"She's my daughter and you will not go after her," he commands as if I am his child, too.

"I don't understand what just happened here?" I stammered with confusion in my tone and unsure whether to go or stay. "Lily had a most wonderful day with me and I wanted her to feel like a girly girl. All she wanted to do was please you as I do, and you've crushed that child's soul," I said, trying to defend myself.

"You're out of line, Sep! It will always be my decision on what is appropriate or not for my daughter. The nerve of the two of you to traipse into my house thinking it's okay for her to look like a tramp? Her goddamn soul isn't *crushed*, as you so aptly state, and she'll have to learn how to manage disappointment in life. She dealt with her mother's death, didn't she?" he said with callousness.

"Where is this coming from?" I asked, my body trembling. "Your anger, Teddy—where is it coming from? Did something happen at the office today?"

"How dare you question me like I'm one of your fucked-up students?" Teddy blurted out with contempt. "Lily is a child walking around with a hairstyle like she's going to a senior prom."

"Teddy," I pleaded. "It's a Saturday night and she isn't going to school with an updo. We had a beautiful girls' day, and if you're so disappointed about her hair you could have spoken to me privately. Now Lily will think that I allowed her to do something that made you mad at her. Blame it on me, but please don't crush her spirit."

"I'm done discussing this and if you keep pressing me in this conversation you can stay home tonight with her," he scolded.

I hate myself! I hate myself at this moment for allowing him to make me feel low and small. I hate myself for allowing him to treat me like his underdog and not his equal. He takes my common sense, the things I am so right about, and shoves it down my throat. I'm inclined to pull every last curl out of my updo, tell him to go fuck himself, and drive to his party without me. He needs a swift foot up his ass, without lubricant, to prove to him I'd rather spend Saturday night with Lily than be with a nasty, condescending asshole. My dream of going to his event in the Blue Room is magnified in my head, bigger than life! Is it worth eating crow?

Quietly I climb the stairs to get ready for the evening, after sitting alone in the den to compose my thoughts. I can hear the humming of the shower in our bedroom. Softly, I tap twice on Lily's bedroom door and then enter. Lily is sitting on the edge of her bed holding Huey Unicorn, her face smeared from crying and her long hair tangled in knots from pulling her hairdo apart. The bobby pins are hanging from strands of hair and Lily looks like a character from a sci-fi movie.

Kneeling down on the floor in front of her, I apologize and carefully remove the pins from her hair.

"Lily, you're my princess girl and you looked absolutely charming. I couldn't think of a better way to spend the day. Oh, Lily girl, I loved every minute with you. Thank you for being with me. Daddy loves you so very much and don't ever forget that. Dry your eyes, sweet girl, dry your eyes."

After reaching for her hairbrush on the nightstand, I prop myself up on the bed sitting cross-legged behind her and begin brushing her lush hair. I can still hear the humming of the shower and I negotiate the amount of time I can stay in her room. If I crawl under Teddy's skin, he will, for sure, leave the house without me.

A short time passes and the shower turns off.

My hands are trembling and my heart is palpitating! Sweat is forming above my brows.

Propelling myself off the bed I kneel in front of Lily.

"Lily, honey, please pack your overnight bag for your sleepover," I tell her, holding her face in the palms of my hands. "I have to get ready now."

"I love you, Seppie."

"And I love you, Sweet Pea."

I walk out quietly, close the door behind me, and gingerly meander into our bedroom, not knowing what to expect from Teddy.

CHAPTER 11

A Weekend to Remember

Teddy is standing by the wardrobe in his burgundy robe and sheepskin slippers. His Hugo Boss suit is laid out on the bed, Ferragamo shoes in its box on the floor. As always, he will look like a million bucks and women will fawn over him, but there will be only one special lady on his arm.

"Undress in front of me," Teddy demands, pulling me in close to his body.

He drops his robe to the floor and there isn't a thing I wouldn't do to make him happy. He and I have powerful chemistry and I assume all relationships take time to fully develop. With Lily losing her mother, I should understand Teddy wanting to be the sole decision maker in everything and anything that relates to their daughter. Still, I want to address the enormity of what transpired downstairs while he's in an endearing mood, but past experience cautions me that he has the propensity to explode. I'll allow this episode to slide and not perseverate on how shitty I feel, because I appreciate his ability to let go of a situation that could have impacted our weekend. Perhaps I should have asked for his permission to style Lily's hair before making that decision. I'll know better next time.

Teddy turns the lock on the doorknob, then approaches me, his strong hands grabbing my shoulders, pushing me down and directing me to kneel in front of him to perform fellatio. Oh yes, I'll pull out all the stops to satisfy him.

My hands stroke him gently and it doesn't take long to get him hard. Guiding him into my mouth at an angle where I can consume all of him, I pull gently on his scrotum. He writhes and moans and there is nothing more satisfying than knowing I'm in the ultimate position of control.

"No woman like you. Never letting go of you, Seppie."

The sweetness that touches my tongue signals that he's on the brink of an orgasm, and I gaze up at his glassy eyes and slow my technique.

Knowing we are short on time to leave the house, my vindictive side takes over and I delight in frustrating him. Passive-aggressive? Perhaps.

"Damn you. You're my bitch!"

His impatience forces him to grab my head, tousle my hair, and rhythmically control the speed that he enters and exits my mouth.

Yes, now I'm all in to the finish.

"Seppie, Seppie, oh, oh, Sepp," he squeaks as he lets himself go.

He pulsates fiercely and I stay in position until he softens. When my mouth detaches, he's pleased that I've absorbed all of him, and I just want to maintain that closeness.

"Teddy, will you lay next to me in the bed, just for a few minutes? We need this."

"Seppie, I need a solid uninterrupted fifteen minutes to get ready."

Giving me a pat on my head, like his dutiful puppy, he walks away and disappears into the bathroom. I feel like a call girl, minus the cash on the dresser.

In less than fifteen minutes he looks as dapper as ever and calls for Lily to grab her things and get into his car. His drive to her best friend's house gives me uninterrupted time, too, to get ready for our spectacular evening.

The new Bobbi Brown lip color looks amazing and was well worth my time at the cosmetics counter.

"Whew!"

I take a deep breath and begin dressing in my sexiest Agent Provocateur undergarments and thigh highs. Teddy will get a sneak preview of what's under my dress, which will, undoubtedly, entice him for the duration of the party.

I've spent way more than I should and ordered a Simone Pérèle silk camisole and boy shorts to sleep in. My overnight bag has been packed for over a week and all I can think about is the Blue Room.

Twenty minutes have passed and the roar of the garage door tells me that we'll be leaving shortly. I slide into my heels and grab my overnight bag.

Standing at the top of the staircase I call for Teddy to carry my bag down the stairs and within seconds, he appears at the foot of the stairs.

With a look of astonishment, he rests his elbow on his hip, covers his mouth with his hand, and shakes his head.

"Mm, now that's what I'm talkin' about!"

Teddy climbs the stairs and I open my legs slightly, showing him what he can expect.

He grabs the bag, and I follow behind him. Blue Room, here I come!

Our car ride to Manhattan was peaceful and we listened to Andrea Bocelli and Sarah Brightman's rendition of "Con Te Partirò." The traffic on a Saturday evening is a challenge, but we left more than enough time to valet the car and settle our belongings at The Beaumont before hailing a cab to The Headless Horseman.

Just short of reaching the hotel Teddy double parked in front of The Headless Horseman to be sure that the Blue Room is ready to accept his guests. Rolling down the passenger side window I have a bird's-eye view of the restaurant's bar area through their large picture window.

"The only thing the bar area will be missing tonight is Seppie," I say with a laugh.

The January chill numbs my cheeks. I quickly roll up my window and impatiently wait for Teddy. After what seems like an eternity, Teddy returns to the car and we're finally on our way to the hotel.

"Is everything set up and ready to go, Teddy?"

"Yep, all good!"

We reach The Beaumont shortly before seven o'clock and a stout parking attendant opens my door and offers me his hand. The doorman guides us through the large etched glass doors and the beauty of the lobby is overwhelming.

"Seppie, wait for me in the sitting area while I check us in," he says, pointing to the moss green velvet chairs that are arranged around a gorgeous swan sculpture.

With a sigh of relief, I release the emotional energy expended on planning for this night.

Ten minutes pass and Teddy returns with the room key.

"And...we're ready to go." Teddy waving the key card in the air.

We stroll to the elevator, my arm looped in his. Intuition tells me that all eyes are on us, but I look straight ahead with harmless arrogance. Once in the elevator he nudges me against the side panel and presses his lips flush against mine. It's moments like this that make all of his depraved qualities dissipate.

The ding of the elevator breaks our momentum on the thirty-seventh floor and we exit to find our room. Room 3717 is at the far end of the hallway with no other rooms adjacent to it. The key card releases the latch and the door opens to a corner suite with an unobstructed view of the Hudson River. In the sitting area, the marble cocktail table is set with a bottle of Veuve Clicquot, chocolate-covered strawberries and pineapple, petit fours, and dainty sandwich triangles.

The window looks out to a winter wonderland and I'm enamored with the beauty of our evening, wishing we had arrived earlier to enjoy each other before heading to The Headless Horseman.

Teddy creeps up behind me and removes my coat.

"Sep, I want this night to be memorable and planned this little surprise."

"I'm speechless and tonight could not be more perfect," I responded, complimenting his efforts. "I'm so in love with you. You know that, don't you?"

"And I with you, Seppie. It's getting late so I'm heading out now to the event. It will take some time to hail a cab and make my way over there."

Feeling nausea in the pit of my stomach, could I be hearing his words correctly? I'm dizzy and when I look at him, he is serving up a crooked smile.

"You look so beautiful," he said, and places a kiss on my lips. "I won't be back too late. Enjoy the food and champagne and be ready to accompany me to a posh little place downtown for after-hours cocktails. I've reserved a table."

"Am I not...?" I started to stammer.

"Sep," he said in my mid sentence, "I never mix my business with my personal life, but I will make this a night for you to remember. Yes?"

He wrapped the Burberry scarf around his neck, winked, and turned to leave the hotel room without giving me an opportunity to respond.

Pacing the patterned carpet, I lost track of time. This morning I woke up and had the world by the balls yet in a flash, he rearranged my universe. Just like that, everything is in disarray. He yanked the magic carpet out from under me and snatched the halo off my head.

Feeling sick to my stomach I made frequent visits to the bathroom where I alternated vomiting with perching myself on the toilet. Any sustenance in my body was evacuated.

"Lily, Lily," I cried out, "I want to pull out my curls, too! Why, oh why, is he so difficult?"

In my relentless rant, I punched my fist into the mattress as hard as I could and two of my beautiful nails cracked. I feel ugly. What was the point of fussing and packing and buying and fantasizing?

"Ugly girl, ugly girl!" I shouted at my image in the mirror. "*You*, Cinderella, are not good enough to go to the ball. The princesses will dance around Teddy because Seppie isn't there."

"Why, oh why, oh why," I wailed.

Exhaustion eventually consumed me and I fell asleep in my crème suede pumps and dreamed; dreamed about the Blue Room. In my dream I show up at The Headless Horseman and wait by the bar. Teddy eventually walks out of the Blue Room to find me sipping a cocktail. After kissing me on the forehead he takes my hand and asks me to join him.

"September, lovely September, everyone is waiting to meet you. This will be a night to remember."

And as we stood in front of the doors to the Blue Room I looked down at my bare feet. The doors opened and I woke up.

My dress is crumpled and the fitted matching dress jacket is underneath me. I roll to the side to pull it out from under my back and walk to the closet for a hanger. There's a spot of blood on the fabric and I realize it's from my nail that is broken down to the skin. Skin. I must have very thick skin to still be in this hotel room dressed up with nowhere to go, waiting for a man who plays with my emotions. The bathroom mirror is very telling of a sad situation. My makeup is a mess and I have a deep line down one side of my cheek from sleeping on the edge of my purse.

"What's wrong with you September Sara Webb?" I ask in a creepy voice staring into the mirror. "Do you think you deserve this? Why do you stay? Desperation? Why, September, do you insist on being this madman's puppet?"

I'm reminded of my junior high school years and the importance of feeling connected at any cost, even if it meant sacrificing my self-esteem.

CHAPTER 12

The Last Supper

I've been living in Teddy's house for the past three years and have accepted his reasons for separating his home life from work, so I no longer fuss with him about going to the Blue Room. Tonight we traveled together to The Beaumont, he in his suit and I in my shearling coat and jeans. Manhattan stores stay open late so Teddy peeled off five hundred-dollar bills and told me to treat myself to a present then await his return to the hotel. A successful attorney by day and a chef in the evening, I'm blessed to have Teddy.

Hailing a taxi, I'm on my way to browse the stores by The Headless Horseman. Inquisitiveness still gets the better of me and I pray curiosity doesn't kill the cat. Walking by The Headless Horseman is my first stop.

The taxi drops me off a block away so I can scope the surroundings, in case Teddy has stepped out to smoke a cigar. Pulling up my collar I stand by the picture window looking much like an Eskimo, and feel that lump in my throat wondering if Teddy's associates ask about me. I'm certain they must since he and I live together.

Silly girl, of course they do, but I'm his best-kept secret!

Swallowing hard I recognize the naivete in my thinking, however I'm of the ilk that people are honest, especially my Teddy.

Shortly before ten I return to The Beaumont with a Bloomingdale's Medium Brown Bag in my hand. The chartreuse rabbit fur hat is for me, the rabbit mittens for Lily. Once upstairs, I draw a bath and settle into our hotel room for the remainder of the night. Watching old movies has been my routine before I go to sleep. I would love to chat with friends and play catch-up, but fear their criticism if asked why I am alone in a hotel room and not at Teddy's event.

Lights out.

"Wake up, sleepyhead," he says softly.

Room service has already been delivered and our morning is spent making love and sharing the special breakfast items on the cart. On the dresser, I notice that Teddy remembered to bring me pastries from the Blue Room's dessert tray.

"I love the marzipan cookies and the black and whites!"

"Only the best for my girl. I asked the waiter to set aside one of each of all the assorted pastries."

"Thank you, love."

My Teddy thinks of everything.

Our drive home from our romantic weekend in Manhattan, the infamous weekend that also allows him to attend his annual holiday party, is peaceful. I'm filled with excited anticipation to see Lily and give her the mittens. It pleases him that I'm attentive to his daughter, but his remark about spending

$145 on mittens for a child didn't sit well with me. He simply doesn't grasp that all acts of kindness soothe any jealousy she might feel. Explaining this to him will predictably spark an argument, so my plan is to surprise her after dinner and not mention it to him again. I tossed a few of the French soaps into my purse to bring Lily and her friend for when we pick her up at her bestie's house.

We pull into Abigail's driveway and Lily is already waiting by the front door with her rolling bag. I step out of the car to retrieve her.

"Thank you, Antoinette, for having Lily for an overnight."

"My pleasure and please, call me Toni," she said warmly.

I removed the soaps from my purse and both girls beamed to get a little gift.

"Toni, I promise to take them for manicures one day during the week."

Lily throws her arms around me then hugs her friend goodbye as Teddy waves from the car.

All of us settle at home after the busy weekend and Teddy will prepare dinner, customary on Sunday evenings.Dinner is always well thought out, and he takes great pride in his culinary skills, parallel to those of a five-star restaurant. I would be inclined to take more initiative to try my hand at cooking, but from what Teddy has shared, Tessa's cooking would be a hard act to follow. My contribution? I initiate uplifting conversation at the dinner table.

When my children were younger, I encouraged each of us to share the best part of our day. Despite life's daily annoyances, ending the day on a positive note is peaceful.At Teddy's table I inspire the three of us to reflect, unwind, and feel that our day had importance. The mood during dinnertime is contingent upon Teddy's temperament. Tonight, unfortunately, nothing of value was brought to the table and Teddy was in a foul mood. Why? Who knows? His demeanor can quickly change with no provocation.

The Last Supper, I shall call it. And as I regurgitate the details of this disappointing night one will agree that The Last Supper is quite fitting. An antique dining room table exquisitely displays a feast prepared with Teddy's good intentions, but he has a bad seed that lives in his belly—the belly of the beast. It is mind-boggling to watch his disposition transform from contentment to fury without warning. Heroic attempts to gain any modicum of decency for myself became my focus..

Teddy's cooking skills are crafted from years of watching Tessa, so I've been informed. Being a simple cook has made me gun-shy, but I can create the finest salad imaginable! I prompted Lily to offer her father assistance in the kitchen and she endured his disapproval during the most basic of tasks, making her feel burdensome. Meeting his standards falls short of impossible so I ask Lily to step around to the other end of the kitchen counter and I hand her an orange.

"Lily, can you please put the finishing touches on the salad?"

She fumbles to peel off the skin with her fingers and adds the sections to the bowl with a look of pride on her face.

"Lily," scolded Teddy, "that orange is pitifully mangled and a perfectly good piece of fruit is ruined!"

"An orange is sometimes hard to peel, but our salad needed that wonderful addition!" I interjected, rushing to Lily's defense.

Her eyes light up as though I am her savior who has thrown her a life raft. Teddy ignores my response, and Lily and I carry the bowl to the table.

Multiple times I attempted to artfully dress the dinner table, but Teddy made it impossible for me to collect the dinnerware from the cabinets during his food preparation.

"Can you move out of my way?" he snapped.

My efforts to set the table ceased, after he became rude and confrontational. I loitered by the door between the dining room and the kitchen until it was safe to resume the task. One is never efficient enough or smart enough when he is in his mood. Lily and I are like mice in a maze going around and around. These moments with Teddy are destructive and escalate quickly so I refrain from engaging in his craziness.

We all take our usual seats at the table and we're ready to enjoy what I must say is truly a beautiful spread. Lily begins to transfer five pieces of roast from a platter to her plate leaving a trail of gravy on the tablecloth while en route.

"Damn it, Lily, only take what you know you can finish," Teddy bellowed. "If you weren't so quick to pile the food onto your plate you wouldn't have made a mess!"

Each morsel of expertly prepared food is poorly digested with Teddy's constant hammering with damaging comments, and then Lily's gloomy behavior that follows. As frequently as he berates her, her behavior deteriorates at the same alarming rate. They cling to their pattern of disquieting behavior.

Lily has begun to show subtle signs of oppositional conduct and I believe she has found her subculture with a group of belligerent girls at school. I put my best foot forward when it comes to guiding Lily in a positive direction. Teddy's behavior, sometimes intolerable at best, doesn't recognize that Lily has stepped off the merry-go-round and doesn't want to listen to him. I see it, but he doesn't.

Teddy is clearly indifferent. A man of great intellect who has lost some sense of order and peace both within himself and with his child, presumably since Tessa passed away. His hope for a brighter tomorrow must have been buried deep in the dirt with their home's For Sale sign, encouraging others to buy his gloomy life. After months of parading strangers through his home as they peeked into the nooks and crannies, Teddy said he removed the sign and decided to keep the house.

His impulsiveness and unaddressed anger spiral out of control without provocation and his audience is left speechless. The tragedies of his past have made him impatient, or perhaps it's an undiagnosed emotional weakness, wearing him thin like an old horse struggling to pull the wooden cart. Behind his beautiful eyes, the discontent is visible as his unkind words pierce through those closest to him like a steely edged knife. Spewing his venom, we are held in a place of unimportance.

My attempt to redirect the tenor of the conversation at the dinner table is hopeless. Teddy disregards me when I ask Lily to share with us the best part of her weekend. No one wins. The vitality of this young girl is suppressed and neither of us feel a sense of worth. I am spoken to disrespectfully as though I were his child, in front of his child. The food crawls up my throat as I rethink my purpose at this table, in this home, and with Teddy. The force that keeps me here negotiates that position, so I function within the confines of this dysfunctional family unit. A reminder, I am also here for Lily.

Throughout dinner I watch her squirm in his presence, often mimicking his comments under her breath to parrot what he sounds like, then Teddy snaps back. Her every move is scrutinized by her father with no room for error.

Dinner hour is finished, and Lily asks to be excused to retreat to her bedroom.

"I'm done, Dad. Can I go upstairs?" she asks without emotion.

"First, young lady, carry your plate to the sink, rinse it, and put it in the dishwasher."

Her belly is full and she is very happy to disengage.

I wait until Teddy gets up from the table, then follow him into the kitchen. It is my call to assist with cleanup.

The pots and pans are under Teddy's watchful eye for cleanliness and the items either going into or staying out of the dishwasher are questioned. A lunatic is looming over me like a dark cloud.

"Why the fuck are you drying that plate with a filthy dish towel? What the fuck is wrong with you?" he screams in my ear.

The heavens opened.

"What are you talking about...?" I step back from him.

"That dish towel was on the floor to clean up spilled water," he says with a twisted look on his face, taking a step toward me.

"I'm sorry, I thought it just dropped..."

"Thought? That's the problem, you don't look or think!"

Without challenge I throw the dish towel on the floor and make my way upstairs. After gathering a few of my belongings from our bedroom I scurry back down the stairs.

Looking back, Lily is halfway down the stairs and peering through the banister.

Blowing her a kiss, I put my finger up to my lips to hush her, and quietly exit through the front door. Walking out temporarily frees me from the monster. I remember feeling this small so many times in my life.

"This is my last supper," I recite to myself as I step away from the house and look up at Lily's bedroom window. "Oh Lord, what should I do?" It has become a hardship to negotiate with Teddy on so many levels.

I tossed my overnight bag in the back of my car, and drove without direction with hopes that Teddy will call me once he realizes that I'm gone. After half a mile I pull to the side of the road so I'm close to home if he calls, recline the seat, and listen to music.

Thoughts rumble around in my head, reflecting on my teenage years, having a first boyfriend, and also being a young wife. There were situations in all of my relationships when I felt powerless. Is it possible that other women have felt this way and tried to work through the rough patches like I have, or did they just walk away? Am I seeking perfection, which doesn't exist? Should I weigh out the good and the bad and choose the column that's easiest to contend with?

Again, how I'm feeling on the inside isn't always in sync with how I present myself on the outside, and my bark is always bigger than my bite. It's my innate unwillingness to step out on the ledge and stand my ground for fear that my other half won't talk me down from it. Lack of confidence precludes it and I visualize standing on that ledge with a person behind me who doesn't give a shit if I jump. This is why I concede and these thoughts are my own insecurity and skewed sense of self.

A sudden echo of knuckles knocking on the window jostles me!

I've fallen asleep in the driver's seat and a police officer is staring at me like I'm homeless. When I roll down the window his uniform immediately intimidates me.

"License and registration, ma'am. Are you all right?" he said austerely.

"Oh yes, officer. I was coming home from a long drive from Upstate New York and exhaustion got the best of me," I replied, thinking quickly on my feet and nervously removing the documents.

Officer Krause, as it reads on his badge, went back to his car to check that I wasn't an escaped felon, then returned within a few minutes.

"Very well, are you okay to drive? There's a motel a half mile on down Esplanade Turnpike," he said, returning my documents and buying my line of bullshit.

"Thank you, Officer Krause, I'll follow your advice."

Krause waited in his police car until my car pulled away from the curb. Once I reached the corner and turned onto Esplanade I noticed his patrol car wasn't behind me and made my way home.

The house is completely dark from the outside with no front lights on. The flashlight from my phone helped me to find the keyhole and I let myself back in. Feeling sadness and pity, for myself, took over as I climbed the stairs quietly, like a burglar. Lily is fast asleep and I step into her bedroom to kiss her forehead before going into our bedroom. Teddy is also fast asleep. Covertly I slide in under the covers next to him after I drop my clothes to the floor. He smells good and his body warms the bed. How nice it would have been to get his call asking me to come home, and apologizing for his poor behavior. But his call never came and I reconcile that Teddy has issues that I can't remedy. He is unable to save me, and so I stay off the ledge.

The morning sun brings us a new day. All is forgotten as he climbs on top of me. Teddy still loves me.

He has us booked for a trip to Italy.

CHAPTER 13

A Place at the Table

The coolness of the small oak chair underneath my legs feels good. I had been told that Italian women dress up in the evening when they saunter out for gelato or espresso, wearing elegant high-heeled shoes for the occasion. I splurged for a chic pair of four-inch sandals to accentuate my enviable height, intending to portray a sophisticated traveler. The luxury of traveling with Teodoro, my Italian American lover fluent in the language and eager to reconnect with his familial roots in a medieval town, would undoubtedly provide a journey that no tour guide could offer.

Teddy is the shining star that tumbled out of the sky to capture my heart, my cupid. In my wildest dreams I never could have imagined romance as fulfilling as it is today. Our nine days of travel, no Lily in tow, will be a fairy tale come true. Agerola, a small town tucked away within the province of Campania, welcomes this divorced Jewish American woman.

I carry my cultural and religious differences in a sleek leather purse to this foreign corner of the world where this experience will exceed all expectations and move me so deeply.

This small sturdy oak chair has supported generations of family through mealtimes and misfortunes and has welcomed many guests as though they were kin. Today, I am kin. At one thirty on a Wednesday afternoon I am seated among four generations of family to share a lovingly prepared dinner comprised of provisions from their farm. Uncle Pasquale's hands are coarse from hard manual labor and his eyes, set deep within his facial lines, show pride as all enjoy the creations from his efforts. Isabella, his five-year-old granddaughter, squirms about on his lap, her fingers affectionately stroking his face. She quickly checks on the plastic puppet in her doll carriage and then playfully takes turns sitting on everyone's lap. They say it takes a village to raise a child.

The aroma from the kitchen momentarily diverts my attention, a cue that a feast is about to begin. Women take turns bustling in and out of the kitchen, stained aprons attached to their rotund bodies. The endless assortment of traditional cuisine is overwhelming, and gathering around this wooden table is the core of their culture. Dinner concludes when limoncello, their customary after-dinner drink, is poured into miniature glasses. Though the language is a hurdle, expressions are easily read and their intermittent touches to my arms and hands have now become a universal language.

When Jack was younger and Sadie was away at college, I would typically prepare a simple dinner for both of us. One of his favorites was coconut chicken with a side of spiral pasta with butter, accompanied by microwavable corn in a cream sauce. In warmer weather, I bought fresh corn and he mastered sucking every kernel of corn from its sleeve. He has become a legend for that skill! When Jack reached the age of fifteen, pulling toward his independence and treasuring newfound freedom with his peers, I had grown to cherish our modest dinners while trying to read his eyes from across the table when conversation grew slim. During those moments I felt disconnected, and information given to me was on a "need to know" basis. It was a struggle to remember the last time all four dining room chairs were occupied and I often wondered if Jack still considered those chairs a family unit. With Sadie away at school, the familial experience had dwindled to a select number of hours per week. Evenings that Jack wasn't home I'd prepare a light supper and settle on the couch with a paper napkin across my lap. The voices from the TV were a distraction, one that curtailed the gentle reminder that my home front was less than adequate.

This was certainly not part of a young girl's dream married in her early twenties. The plan for a traditional family constellation, that their dad and I discussed before we exchanged vows, disappeared at our yard sale with other household items, during the divorce. Paralleling this Italian family experience in Agerola creates an ache, but at this moment I am the queen of Italy with high-heeled shoes sitting on a sturdy oak chair.

This Italian family exemplifies a life that is rich with simplicities; my life has not been simple for a long time. Teddy's experience here is bittersweet, as he connects with his culture, one that is lost in America. His hazel eyes show sadness, and with a heavy heart I place my hand on his shoulder to communicate that I understand the pain of a shattered family.

Conversely, this family has captured the beauty of intactness, as it exists here. I fantasize about sharing this experience with my children; selfishly hoping they will invite them for a visit with me. Then guilt sets in that Lily has never sat on this small oak chair.

My smile is from ear to ear. Cousin Carlotta has been eloquently translating my appreciative sentiments from English to their beautiful Italian language.

The wine, served in small glass pitchers, is pressed from the grapes in their vineyards. The olive trees are picked clean late in the year and pressed during the months from November through February. Figs, plums, and apples multiply on the trees and a variety of vegetables sprout up from the ground. When I remove my sandals, my feet connect with the rich soil of a farm that has been passed down for decades. Strolling through the acreage and rapidly snapping pictures of Aunt Lucia tugging ripe zucchini from the earth and placing them in her satchel, I recognize that photos cannot capture the splendor of this afternoon. The trees are bursting with plump, ripe figs. I reach for one and with each bite, the sizzling sun dries the juice on my hand, yet what I savor in my mouth is the fruit of their dedication to labor-intensive work.

A few yards away chickens scurry about as they are gathered into their pens. Ambling through the grass and dirt patches I enter the wooden fence that contains them. Oh my, I feel like an intruder as I witness a chicken dropping her eggs into a rectangular nest of hay.

"Puoi tenerla se vuoi!"

Graciously, Uncle Pasquale places a chicken in my hands and her body feels warm when I hold her against my chest. In a few weeks the chicken will serve her purpose for a family meal. Squeezing her firmly there's a reluctance to release her;

for once the chicken is set free so is the moment.

A small, two-bedroom furnished cottage just a few yards away from Aunt Lucia became my and Teddy's home away from home during our visit. The freshly cut flowers artfully arranged in a large mason jar welcomes us after an arduous drive down a scenic Adriatic highway. Our day was filled with food, family, and emotion. Impeccable thought went into a stocked refrigerator of curious soft drinks in tiny bottles, fresh fruit, and other staples intended to tide us over during our downtime. Each window boasts a quaint view of the other small cottages on pencil-narrow streets, and the small double doors on the cottage's lower level open to a private patio, complemented by the most aromatic flowers in full bloom.

When the sun was put to bed, so was I. The evening breeze pushed against the wooden shutters, demanding our attention as they clanked against its frame. Though I restlessly lay awake until the wee hours of the morning that time was well spent reflecting on a timeless day. The shrieking of the roosters and a neighbor calling to another from her window roused me from my few hours of slumber. I pull myself away from the white linens and shuffle my feet to the bedroom window, leaning out to embrace the breaking of a new day.

Aunt Lucia, speaking only Italian, is in her early eighties with an angelic, porcelain face. Her front door stays ajar for early morning coffee and biscuits, and on a particular morning I visit her when Teddy leaves for his early walk.

"*Buongiorno*, Settembre!"

"*Buongiorno, zia* Lucia."

I'm escorted to the couch where we sit quietly while the milk steams on the stove. Aunt Lucia cups my hands in hers and we gaze at each other, our eyes communicating more effectively than if we understood the other's language. This moment speaks volumes, touching my heart in ways that I cannot articulate.

The coffee smells aromatic. Aunt Lucia kisses the top of my head, then slowly makes her way to the kitchen with an awkward gait. I follow behind her and once she assembles our breakfast on the shellacked wooden serving tray, I carry it to the table. She and I enjoy each other's presence and she smiles warmly as I help myself to a second biscuit from the silver tin. As quickly as I see her smile, the sides of her mouth turn down and her eyes look sad.

Confounded, I wonder if I've done something to disappoint her and reach for her hand. She grasps it firmly and gestures me to stand up. Aunt Lucia gently tugs me along and I follow her into the small spare bedroom. The walls are painted sage green and the twin bed is made up nicely with an immaculately ironed cotton duvet.

She motions to me to sit down.

I watch, with curiosity, as she walks to the closet and slides one of the ceiling-high doors open, exposing her collection of housecoats on fabric hangers. On the right side of the closet are built-in shelves where she reaches for a canvas bag.

She joins me on the bed and removes a picture album. The front reads, *Teodoro e Tessa*, and it's obvious that she wants me to look through pictures of Teddy with his late wife. It would be more appropriate for Teddy to share the album, but I'm riddled with curiosity.

Before Aunt Lucia opens the album, she crosses her hands over the leather-bound cover and hangs her head. A tear falls from her eye and I'm working hard to decipher her emotion with the utmost sensitivity. Helplessly she lifts her head and throws her hands up as if to say, "What has happened?"

The very first page shows Teddy and Tessa's wedding picture, which sparks a tinge of jealousy, wishing that he and I were photographed. Tessa is a natural beauty, minimalistic, with an olive complexion needing nothing more than a hint of rouge and lipstick. Her eyes are huge with a warm brown hue that can easily draw the attention of admirers. On their special day they are gazing at each other in adoration. The pages that follow are random in years, however I'm startled to see that Tessa's appearance progressively deteriorates, looking as frail as the frayed yellowed pages.

Aunt Lucia turns to the album's final page and her pudgy hands tremble slightly as she lifts up a small picture from the adhesive backing, some of the old adhesive ripping off a piece of the photo. Tessa looks pale, almost ill, and has Lily sitting on her lap. Lily looks, maybe, five or six years old and Tessa appears explicitly different from when she was married. Was Tessa's illness rapidly progressing at this point?

Aunt Lucia places the photo in an envelope that has Tessa's name and return address, obviously sent by Tessa.

She hands me the envelope.

"Conservare in un luogo sicuro. Per favore, conservare in un luogo sicuro!"

"I don't understand? What should I do with this?"

"Conservare in un luogo sicuro," she pleads.

Sicuro sounds like *secure,* so I carefully place the picture in my pocket.

"Zia Lucia? *Zia* Lucia? *Settembre? Dove sono le mie ragazze?"* calls Teddy. Aunt Lucia's face loses color and she quickly places the album and the canvas sack in the dresser drawer that is closest to her. She was shaking like a fifty-cent ladder.

When she and I stood up to leave the bedroom, I pushed the picture deeper into my pocket, then Teddy appeared in front of us at the doorway.

I smile.

Each day that followed was as memorable as the day prior and my dream of enjoying a gelato in high-heeled shoes was also fulfilled. The purchase, however, was not made in a fancy shop on a lively street showcasing the ladies in their stylish attire. It was a complimentary gelato from Cousin Lorenzo, owner of a tiny store on a remote street that one could easily miss if not for the dim light behind the wooden-framed screen door. We sat outside on wobbly white resin chairs eating the best gelato in the world. I examined the sky, musing that life is so different from place to place although everyone settles under the same stars.

On our departure day at six o'clock in the morning, every family member gathered at Aunt Lucia's home to bid us farewell. I removed my high-heeled shoes before loading the car, feeling the earth beneath my feet as a reminder of Agerola. As we organized our belongings in the tiny, powder blue, compact rental car I considered the items in my suitcase and the additional room that I saved for souvenirs. The extra space was still in my suitcase, and the special things I was carrying home were in my heart. Teddy pulled the car away from the curb to make our way down the dark narrow street. I clutched my high-heeled shoes, realizing I traveled a distance that cannot be measured in days.

CHAPTER 14

The Blue Room Revisited

Settled into the routine at the Zezza household I thought about selling my Manhattan apartment, but after careful consideration I decided it would be best to keep it as our weekend getaway with the option to rent it at any time. We have the best of both worlds, a house in the suburbs and a beautiful apartment in the city. However, it is an ongoing battle to inspire Teddy to have an occasional overnight rendezvous, and he digs his heels in about leaving Lily for "no good reason." He's adamant about staying put in his Greenwich house, and that is what we do.

Sadie and Jack spend time with us as a family, having casual barbecues in the backyard or meeting them out at a restaurant. Both situations seem to work well. Teddy's outbursts are contained and never occur in my children's presence, or in the presence of outsiders. He displays the best version of himself and can sell someone ice in the winter. If my children were to observe, or hear about, his insolent behavior toward me, they would frown upon our relationship and lose respect for my judgment. In my own defense, no one knows him the way that I do.

There are so few of Teddy's friends and family who I've engaged with throughout the time we've been together. I adored everyone in Italy, but with a million miles between us it isn't likely we will visit again anytime soon. When we go out on the weekends it is fancy and with Lily. Occasionally he will allow her a sleepover, but mostly she is tethered to us. It surprised me that Lily did not accompany us on our Italy trip and when I questioned him there was no meaningful response. Nonna Martha stayed with Lily at our house which kept him free from worry. I was grateful for the time that we spent alone, not to mention that the intimacy was better than ever!

Tonight is our annual trip to The Beaumont. For years I remained curious about his workplace and those who see him on a daily basis. It's perplexing that his frustration and impatience doesn't rear its ugly head with his partners and co-workers who must know him almost as well as I do. Typically, people spend more time at their jobs than they do with their families. Does he bottle up his anxiety and relieve it at home? In a strange sort of way, I feel special. Because we are so close, he doesn't have the need to filter what comes out of his mouth. I would appreciate an apology from him, more often than not, but he knows I love him regardless.

I've visited his office only once, after-hours, when he needed to retrieve a file. On several occasions, on days I didn't have work, I've offered to bring lunch to his office, but that was vehemently discouraged. Interestingly, the one time that I was in his office there were no pictures of Tessa or Lily on his desk, which struck me as odd. In our first year together, I framed a beautiful picture of him, Lily, and me to place on his desk. He put it in his briefcase, smiled, and said thank you. Several months later when cleaning our bedroom, I found the picture under a shoebox on the floor. Go figure. Well, I know he won't mix business with pleasure so I dismissed my disappointment.

The weather this evening is inclement and it had been snowing on and off during the day. Rather than have Lily sleep at her friend's house, Teddy picked up Nonna Martha and asked her to stay at our house. I knew Lily would be bored, but I promised to take her somewhere special the following day. Lily and I play this game where she jumps into my car, closes her eyes, and when we reach our destination I surprise her by parking in front of one of several of her favorite stores. She's given a pocket calculator and a twenty-dollar bill with thirty minutes to spend as close to that amount as she could. Though Teddy is wealthy, and when with him her purchases are limitless, I believe she enjoys having boundaries. It's mostly about us having fun together and less about the monetary value of what she buys.

I sat on the chaise, by the window in our hotel room, watching the snow blanket over the rooftops. The city glistened and after a certain hour, the hustle and bustle on the streets below seemed to ease. Every January, Teddy books the same hotel room with champagne and a cart filled with sandwiches and fruit, and I wait for his return from the Blue Room. I am still saddened that his work event isn't shared with me because his partners and employees invite their significant others.

This cold weather tends to make me sluggish and it's a relief to not have the burden of dressing to the nines, although I would in a heartbeat. Cozied up with my crossword puzzles and drinking champagne, I fell asleep on the chaise.

A tingling on my outer thigh woke me up, as I accidentally had my phone on vibrate. There are seven missed calls from Lily. It is 8:20 p.m. When I return her call, she sounds frantic.

"Seppie, please come home. I've been calling Dad's cell phone, but it keeps going to voicemail. Please come home!"

"Lily, slow down. First of all, are you alright? Where is Nonna Martha?"

"She's upstairs sleeping, but you need to come home. Tell Dad to come home!"

"Okay, pea. My phone was on vibrate, but I will try to call Dad now. Just be patient and we will come home as soon as we can. Please stay calm."

"Isn't Daddy with you?" she insists. "Why do you have to call him?"

"No, Lily. Dad attends this event by himself. Just sit tight and I'll call him. Do you want to put Nonna Martha on the phone? I'm worried about you."

"No, no," she pleads. "Just hurry home."

Lily ends the phone call and I immediately try to call Teddy. It goes to voicemail. What to do now?

After leaving three voice messages and a dozen text messages, I'm prepared to hail a cab to The Headless Horseman.

"This is just great, fucking great," I chant to myself, "my first arrival to the Blue Room and I'm dressed for a flea market."

I'm not certain I should be going there, but how can he be angry? Lily is hysterical and he is unreachable. Another option is to call the restaurant and have them find him at the party. No, that's not a good idea. Teddy will be alarmed that there's an emergency.

Twenty minutes later makeup is on and the ends of my hair are curled. The black suede boots have noticeable white spots from the salt on the sidewalk so I quickly clean the sides with a washcloth. There's still no return call from Teddy.

A quick text to Lily telling her we will be home soon yields a "KK" response, assuring me that she's all right.

The motion of the elevator ride down to the lobby created slight nausea. I feel sick to my stomach, mostly because of the situation.

"The Blue Room." I mumble, "Dear God, what am I doing?"

The concierge opens the large glass doors and I ask him to hail me a taxi.

"The Headless Horseman, Madison and East Seventy-Seventh."

My breathing is labored and my chest feels as though it is about to explode. The thought of making my grand entrance into the Blue Room temporarily overshadows the real reason for going there. Oh God, I feel like a crazy person.

With my eyes glued to the phone, I feel my legs shaking uncontrollably and knocking into the passenger door. Nothing. Nothing. The roads are slick and the tires skid whenever the driver accelerates at a green light. It's impossible to see the street signs because the snow has covered most of the lettering.

Breathe, Seppie, breathe. That's it, Seppie, in and out. Just breathe.

"Ma'am, we're here. That will be $17.30. You can slide your credit card if you're not paying cash."

"Thank you. I have twenty-two dollars. Keep the change and drive safely."

"Much appreciated and careful getting out."

Of course, I step into a puddle of slush and saturate my boots. What a fucking mess! Careful not to fall, I step onto the sidewalk in front of The Headless Horseman and peer in through the foggy window. The usual cast of characters are at the bar area, but not as crowded as a Thursday night happy hour.

I haven't walked through their front doors since I met Teddy here years ago. The space seems smaller than what I remember. I was sitting at the bar with that expensive bottle of chardonnay chilling in the cooler, wanting so much to be with Teddy. Now I have him and now I have a reason to go into the Blue Room.

"Would you like to check your coat?" asks the maître d'.

"Possibly, thank you. I'll know in just a minute."

Several patrons are still finishing dinner and I'm careful to not knock into their tables as I make my way to the Blue Room.

The infamous Blue Room. I'm actually standing in front of its doors!

My body is rigid. At nine fifteen, surely they are all seated for their dinner.

Here we go, Seppie. Do it!

With each hand folded around the knobs of the double doors I breathe deeply and pull them open.

Darkness.

"There's no one in there. Can I help you?" asks a voice from behind me.

Darkness? This is all a dream.

"Ma'am, can I help you? Are you okay?" asks a waiter, again.

"No, I'm not okay. Would you be so kind to turn on the lights? Please do that for me," I ask softly.

"One moment, let me call over the manager."

My body has separated from my soul. I'm numb and confused with more questions than answers.

"Hello, ma'am. Is there something I can help you with? My waiter said that you would like us to turn on the lights in the Blue Room. Did you leave something behind? I'm the manager."

"The party. Pucchi, Pucchi, and Zezza, the firm? It's their annual after-season holiday party. It's tonight. Every year at this time they book the Blue Room. Please turn on the lights," I insist.

The manager steps inside the Blue Room and flips the light switches one by one. And as he does my jaw drops. I'm speechless.

"Pucchi, Pucchi, and Zezza, the firm. Where is everyone? Is the event over? You must know Teodoro Zezza, yes?"

"I'm so sorry, ma'am, but there was no event in this room tonight. As you can see the chairs are turned upside down on the tabletops. Perhaps you've mistaken this restaurant for another?" he says apologetically.

"Well, what about last year at this time, and the year before that?" I implore. "Pucchi, Pucchi, and Zezza. The firm. Was their event here, in your Blue Room for the past two years? Was it?"

"I am the manager and part-owner of this restaurant, also in charge of the bookings and I don't recall that firm ever scheduling a party in this room. I apologize."

"How do you know? How can you remember? Surely many people have booked this room. Please check. This is so important to me and I would be very grateful if you could just check your records. It's Pucchi, Pucchi, and Zezza. Please, and thank you for your trouble. I'll just wait here by the doors."

"As you wish, but it may take me a while to look through the book."

The manager walked away.

The sound of desperation reverberates throughout my body. I want to step outside of myself because I don't like who I am, who I have become. I'm lifeless, standing inside the doors of the Blue Room. I imagined the clinking of glasses, some dancing, and the pastries that Teddy would bring me from the dessert table. Empty and dark is the infamous Blue Room, synonymous with my place in Teddy's world, empty and dark. Where is Teddy?

Ten minutes later the manager finds me.

"Ma'am, I checked the book, and I'm so sorry. The firm that you mentioned and the person you mentioned have not booked any parties here. I looked as far back as three years for you. Is there something else I can assist you with? Can I call for a cab?" he asked considerately.

My phone was buzzing, and when I pulled it from my pocket Lily's name appeared.

"Hi Lily, honey, I'm on my way home."

"Yes," I said to the manager, "a cab, please."

As he appointed one of his staff to hail a taxi, I scanned the emptiness of the Blue Room one last time before closing its doors. My boots squeaked musically on the wooden floorboards and they seemed to be singing to me, "Go home, Cinderella. There is no prince. Go home."

I walked through the doors of the restaurant for the last time and the mystique of the Blue Room evaporated into the snowflakes.

CHAPTER 15

The Beginning of the End

My recollection of the cab ride home to Lily is naught. I dozed from emotional exhaustion and vaguely remember self-negotiating if I should go back to The Beaumont and await Teddy's instructions or rush to see Lily. My motherly instincts always have me err on the side of tending to the child, which I did, knowing that I'd be in a no-win situation with Teddy. I reached the house shortly before eleven o'clock. and was not happy about the $137.00 cab ride home when Teddy had the car in the city.

Teddy's car wasn't in the driveway, which made me wonder if he had returned to the hotel. Why haven't I heard from him? Why was there no event in the Blue Room? Another woman? No, that's out of the question because he and I live together.

After my fourth attempt on the keypad, the garage door opened. I entered the quiet house and kicked off my wet boots by the door. Hurriedly, I climbed the stairs two steps at a time and could see that Nonna Martha's bedroom door was closed. Approaching the top level, she could be heard snoring heavily. Lily's bedroom door was open, and I tiptoed inside to find her room empty. She was neither in her bedroom nor ours. Puzzled, I checked my phone again, but there was nothing from Teddy.

Descending the staircase, I could hear whimpering at the far end of the house. As I approached the study the sobbing became louder, and I spotted Lily crouched in the corner holding her knees to her chest. When I walked in, she was staring straight ahead in a catatonic state.

"Lily?" I said in a soft tone. "Honey, I'm here with you now. Have you heard from Daddy? Lily. Honey, look at me and tell me what has you so upset?"

She continued to stare straight ahead and sob, and it was difficult to break her concentration.

"Lily, why are you in the study? Were you looking for a book for school? It's late. I never see you in the study and you usually do your schoolwork in your bedroom."

Nothing. Lily is despondent. I walk over to the desk for a clue, anything that will help me decipher what has this child in distress.

On top of the desk is a book called *How to Draw Cartoon Characters* and on the floor is the novel *Atlas Shrugged* by Ayn Rand. I pick up the book from the floor, bring it to Lily, and kneel in front of her.

"Is this the book you were looking for?"

Lily doesn't answer me, but I notice something underneath her thigh and carefully slide it out from under her. It's an article from an Italian newspaper dated almost twenty years ago. The picture shows a young woman in handcuffs standing in front of two police officers. From the pictures that I've seen and the picture that was given to me by *Zia* Lucia, it looks like Tessa. The only word I can decode is *prostituta*. Scanning the words in the article is futile because nothing else is remotely understandable.

After sitting on the floor beside Lily, to comfort her, she finally broke her silence after half an hour.

"That is my mother in the picture," she says through her tears. "Why would they arrest her? I know so little about her life and look at her, she was just a bad person," Lily accuses.

"Sweet girl, surely there is an explanation and a story. Where did you find this article? Has Daddy called you back?" I asked as I checked my phone with no returned calls or messages.

"Daddy has not called back and I don't understand why he's not with you. Where is he and how do we know if he's okay?" Lily barks.

"I'm sure he's fine, Lily. And I'm so sorry, but I don't know where he is. I'm right here and I'm not going anywhere. Please tell me how you found this article?"

"I was pulling out my cartoon book and the book next to it fell out of the bookshelf. The books are all cramped up tight in there. I could barely get my fingers in there to pull it out," she complained.

"Okay, and..."

"And that big book on the floor fell and the article fell out. Read it to me. Tell me what the article says about my mother!"

"I wish I could, sweetheart, but I cannot read Italian. Daddy is the only one who can read it to you."

I allowed Lily to cry in my arms and felt helpless. I could offer no answers and I had as many unanswered questions as

Lily. The loss this child has experienced is unfathomable and the article adds to her injury.

"It's okay, Lily, I'm here with you," I said as my own eyes began to well up with tears. "I wish I could make this not hurt for you."

And in our few minutes of silence, Lily's whimpering slowed to more regulated breathing, then the growling of the garage door disturbed our silence.

We waited for Teddy to enter the house and a fierce range of unprocessed thoughts and emotions ran through my head, getting me to the finish line with no memory of the race. Confusion and fear reign high as I stand on that so-called ledge. In a perfect world he would reach out his hand and tell me to step down from that ledge and feel safe with him; he would tell me that "we're okay" and there's an explanation for where he's been. Tell me that he appreciates my smart decision to come to his daughter's rescue. Tell me that he's comfortable with my independent thoughts and choices, and with that follows respect.

But an overwhelming fear looms over me, breathing on my neck and strangling the air from my lungs. He'll tell me I didn't wait to follow his instructions. He'll tell me his cell phone died and he couldn't find me. He'll say that I infiltrated his business world and snooped around the Blue Room. He'll yell at me for leaving him in the city and taking control of his child. I know the repertoire and he knows I'll back down. The pattern of behavior between us never changes and because of that goddamn ledge, I'm not secure enough to step out on it and stand my ground. Regardless of how skilled I am at communicating my feelings, more of the same never means better. After the hundredth time my words will never generate a different outcome. Regardless of where I think I should be in his life, he will always chain me down to the place that serves him best.

I hear Teddy drop his keys on the counter and shuffle his feet through the kitchen, still wearing his shoes. It's a scene from a horror movie and I'm hiding from a killer who is brandishing a knife.

"Teddy, we're in here, in the study," I call out in a motherly and protective voice. "Lily is in here with me."

Teddy, now standing in the doorway, is looking larger than life: big, scary, and assuming. My sadness and anger prevail. I want his forgiveness for taking the lead and acting on my good intentions. I'm committed to the investment of time to nurture a relationship with both Teddy and Lily so all of us can show the best parts of ourselves while we travel through loss and disappointment. Loss is difficult for adults, and Lily is a fragile baby bird who is falling from the nest. My arms are here to catch her, and I'm sad because this moment feels like the beginning of the end. I'm so damn angry about not allowing myself to be me.

"Lily, come to your father," Teddy says without emotion. Lily has now curled up closer to me.

"Lily!"

"Teddy, can you and I talk in the other room before you speak to Lily?"

"Lily," he says, his tenor is angry and impatient, "come to your father!"

"Teddy, I just calmed her down from something that she discovered. It would be best if you and I could speak alone first, please."

"I'm her father and you are not her mother," he exploded.

"Your services, right now, are not needed."

Tossed to the side like yesterday's trash, I could feel venom creeping up in my throat and the fire in my eyes burning through the litany of emotions.

Rising to my feet I step out on that ledge, now toe-to-toe with my demons.

"I may not be her mother, but this woman is." I raised my tone and held the article in front of him.

Pushing the newspaper clipping in his monstrous face makes me feel good. Good to be on the ledge and on the edge.

"Lily found this article on Tessa and was desperate for you to come home. Nonna Martha is asleep upstairs and doesn't know about any of this. Lily called me when she couldn't reach you and that's when I left a shitload of messages for you. Did you not get them?"

"Curb your mouth in front of my daughter."

"Did...you...get ...my...messages, I'm asking you?" I spoke with controlled anger in my voice.

"If you *must* know, the party room becomes very loud and I don't always hear the ringer," he replied defensively and I could see the veins bulging in his neck.

The blood rushed to my face. That lousy, motherfucking liar has the audacity to blatantly lie. Dumbass Seppie will believe it all, so it's business as usual. How many lies did he tell his wife?

"Sweet Pea, can you go to your bedroom, and I'll be upstairs shortly to tuck you in?'

"Lily, stay where you are. I'm your father!"

"Please, Seppie, put me to bed?" Lily cried.

Lily rushes to my side.

"Lily," Teddy said coarsely, "Seppie won't be putting you to bed tonight. I will tuck you in. Forget about the article because it doesn't matter, Lily. It was a long time ago."

"Daddy, she's my mother and I want to know about her. Read the article to me. I have a right to know."

The floodgates opened and now Lily is back to square one—frantic and crying hysterically.

"Teddy, she has seen the article. Let's try to help her with this. She's trying to connect with her mother's past. Please give her something with your discretion," I pleaded.

"I want you *out*," ordered Teddy. "Leave our house. You're on my property. Get out. I'll send your belongings."

"No, Daddy, no. Seppie, put me to bed."

"Go to your room now, Lily, and don't say another word," yelled Teddy.

Lily ran out of the study and I couldn't go after her. She is not my daughter and this is not my home.

Finally, I'm out on that ledge and the wind is blowing fiercely.

Liar, liar. You fucking liar, I am screaming inside my head, and then realized the words were spilling from my mouth. "There is no party, no event, and no Blue Room. Year after year, nothing happens there, you lying sack of shit! How dare you...you...you put me in this position? Waiting in a hotel room while you lie about your whereabouts. And Lily doesn't understand why you're not with me and I have no answers for her or for myself. Your firm hasn't booked a party in that Blue Room in the past three years, Mr. Zezza, Mr. Fancy-Schmancy Counselor at Law. Where have you been, Counselor Zezza? Where the fuck have you been?" I demanded.

Out of breath, I continue to wail.

"Where have you been, Counselor Zezza, where?"

I've stepped out of my skin and out on the ledge. My parents were serious gardeners who planted me to be this exquisite rose and unselfishly I replanted myself in Teddy's garden. Slowly I stopped blooming because over time he blocked my sunshine and deflowered me. Who am I in this very moment, my body contorting and shaking violently, making me as ugly on the outside as Teddy is on the inside? I'm a mother to my own children, but I'm no one to Lily. I was once a wife to another man, but I'm no one to Teddy. I've deserted the one person I should pay homage to, September. I need to search for September. Without me, there is no other workable relationship. Everything will always begin and end with me.

And the wind carried me off the ledge.

CHAPTER 16

Never Look Back

It is undeniably painful to reminisce about my final hours in Teddy and Lily's house. Standing in the middle of their study and being commanded to leave the premises, like a trespasser, was devastating. I was evicted from a life I had settled into. Was it Lily's worst nightmare to lose her mom and now lose me? I was once a girl her age, vulnerable and relying on the guidance of a mother. How were Lily's hours filled between midnight and dawn? Were her eyes fixated on her bedroom door hoping I would walk through it to tuck her in?

As promised, did her father come upstairs to put her to bed? She sleeps peacefully when she's tucked in with my melodic, "Sweet dreams, Sweet Pea," and then I dim the light and close her door halfway. Lily and I had developed a routine. Did she fall fast asleep, and was she dreaming of me? Did it cross her mind that she was my little girl, too, and that my heart is broken? Both of our worlds are shattered once again.

I'll never be Teddy's other half, and Lily and I will only be a memory to each other. That bastard castrated anything that was good, and like an unskilled surgeon removed a healthy organ. The remnants of his decisions will cripple Lily, manifesting itself in years to come. I'll never see her bloom the way I've watched my children blossom, but beautiful Lily, I'll carry you in my heart.

On that evening Teddy asked me to leave their house and I did, carrying my wet boots in my hands. Once outside, I sat down on the snow-covered lawn to pull them on. I have no memory of walking through the rooms of the house, upon my final exit, or taking inventory of what would no longer be familiar. I left everything behind. It was too painful to collect my clothing and memories, and stuff them into one suitcase and several trash bags. Closing the empty drawers would make me feel sick to my stomach so it was easier, emotionally, to walk out knowing that my presence in their house remained through my possessions. My shoes, oh, my damn shoes; yes, I needed new shoes anyway and a fresh path to walk on.

The seat of my jeans quickly became soaked from the wet snow. When I looked back, Teddy was standing inside the garage watching me, then a few seconds later had disappeared from view as he rolled down the garage door on another chapter of my life. I looked up at the cold gray sky and debris was falling, falling, falling. Falling from the sky with a deafening sound to remind me of how disconcerting my life has really been. Once the fragments settled onto the ground around me a tiny stream of light peeked through the darkness and I thought about the book *Goodnight Moon*. Good night stars, good night air, good night noises everywhere.

All of Teddy's noise and aggressive chatter were eventually

eliminated from my life, and with that Lily's sweet chirping in my ear like little girls do. Teddy robbed me of everything in a surreptitious way, as only a narcissist could. He'd convinced me that he was giving me God's greatest gifts, giving me all of himself with Lily included. All the while he was filling his pockets with my trust, my good intentions, my passion, and my selflessness. In the end he emptied his pockets into the trash, lit a match, and stoked the fire, and had me watch the best parts of myself burn. The agony of being discarded left me fragile and confused. As I stepped back from the flames I felt like a refugee looking for a place to recover. Wide-eyed, I watched the warm, radiant flames die down to sparks, then noticed that something was left behind in the embers, the one thing that would save me.

For the longest time, since our breakup, I yearned for the sensual, loving, and accommodating side of Teddy. My nights alone were agonizing and restlessness stayed with me, like a best friend. Rather than go to sleep at my usual hour I fiddled around until the small hours of the morning, hoping that exhaustion would knock me out cold. No such luck. When I crawled under the bedsheets thoughts of Teddy muddled my brain, replacing silence with his once whispers of sweet nothings. They encroached on my ability to sleep and I found myself longing for his scent on my pillow. His good and evil had me mentally distraught, tied up in knots. I craved him, but in a flash remembered the nights I would cry myself to sleep from his silent treatment, after he laced into me Teddy had his special way of isolating me and making me feel worthless, which I internalized.

Even so, I melted when I would wake up during the night and feel him next to me. He looked peaceful, though I knew his demons were asleep to recharge their batteries. I always took the high road and made amends with him when the morning rolled in, however it never made a difference. Once the dirty water settled to the bottom of the pot it would bubble back up with more frequency as my connection with Lily solidified. It became a vicious cycle, spinning between romance and torment.

A dull ache still nudges me that there's a void, but I no longer memorialize the eroticism of Teddy's and my alone time at The Beaumont. It remains bittersweet when I dredge those memories of sitting alone in a hotel room like a hopeful schoolgirl. And perhaps it's an omen that The Headless Horseman changed ownership and became The Cavern. How apropos? A cavern it is indeed, to bury all of those memories.

Years have passed, and I know nothing of Teddy's or Lily's whereabouts. They fell into an abyss, never having reached out to me in any form. I cannot fault Lily who was under the authority of her father, and communicating with his underage child could have become litigious. Well, life continues and I've learned how to walk again. Time and space have opened my eyes to realities that I once refused to see.

My last image of Teddy was on that snowy night when he shut the garage door as I sat in the snow. For a long time that image of him was mammoth—a powerful and assuming man who seemed larger than life. He reminded me of the fourth card on the Rorschach, the inkblot that can correlate to a figure of a monster. I've Googled a picture of that image and placed it side by side with a picture of Teddy, and after staring long and hard at both images I shrunk Teddy down to size. He is not gargantuan, but a small and dangerous man who has mastered the art of manipulation.

My children are adults, and I've become more absorbed in their day-to-day lives in a gentle, natural, and supportive way. I'm far from being creepy. Sadie loves to use that word and she's the first to say, 'Mom, you're being creepy!' They have their space, but when I spend time with them together, it is heavenly.

Recently Sadie, Jack, and I took a long car ride together to a family event, and as much as I abhor long car rides, I could have driven for days without stopping. We listened to SiriusXM's classic vinyl station and began belting out songs like a bunch of crazy teenagers. My heart was singing higher than my voice and I wanted to apply the child locks and never let them out. My greatest treasures in life were with me, and I was living in the moment.

An hour or so into our trip the conversation between them included music groups that were unfamiliar to me and inside jokes that I wasn't privy to. Several times I tried to interject in their conversation, but felt like the new kid on the block. Their age gap has officially closed and I was no longer the link. By all standards I am still a hip mom, but their conversation threw me into a tailspin. I'm overjoyed that my children have forged a strong bond with each other in ways that a parent can only hope for, but there's this unexpected sadness that emanates from our generation gap. I supposed this is what's to be predicted with age. My stories and comments once humorous and interesting no longer stimulate them, but their kind smiles and chuckles k eep them loving and respectful toward me.

The toughest part of parenting, although one never stops being the parent, is complete. I still take great pride in guiding these two magnificent gifts from God and pinch myself, at times, not believing that these beautiful gems are mine. Though our age gap now seems oceans apart I never have that fear of floating away. With certainty, the life raft is there.

CHAPTER 17

How Does Your Garden Grow?

Seasons come, seasons go, and the hands on my watch rotate methodically around its dial without pause. An unforgiving reminder that we gain wisdom while time ages us. I haven't come to terms with the trade-off, but would like to have had the choice. Pushing into my early sixties, I would barter less wisdom for fewer facial lines. The aging process stalks me and tampers with my external beauty. Like a rabbit, I scurry to make the minor adjustments that keep me looking unchanged from year to year. Minimal amounts of makeup show fewer lines, but with the first hardy smile, the foundation settles into the creases.

One morning, sitting on the toilet, I grabbed the purple hand mirror from underneath the sink to tweeze my eyebrows. As I hung my head to look at my reflection, the skin around my face fell forward and puckered. I stared back at an old woman, reminded of the famous perceptual illusion where the brain switches from seeing a young woman to an old woman. I had this guttural, internal cry.

Go fuck yourself, Father Time! Give me my years back, the fullness in my lips and the elasticity in my skin. Give me back all of the things I have taken for granted, like roasting in the sun during my teenage years never believing that I would age. Hold on there, Father Time! I'm not certain how the years ran away from me, but now I'm chasing them down.

The old adage that youth is wasted on the young holds merit; for it takes nearly a lifetime to understand how we fit into our universe. Once that epiphany hits home our opportunities for do-overs have already dwindled. It's a challenge to get it right the first time. Choices, choices—I have reached that crossroad in my life where I contemplate my choices, both past and present. The choice to stay in a relationship or abandon it, and in most cases I stay because I inherently believe in the power of perseverance. Staying makes me neither a good nor a bad person, just someone who shows commitment beyond reasonable limits. I stay until I realize that I don't have the ability to cut and paste people into situations that I want them to be in. We have control only over ourselves. No regrets, though. I've been on a treasure hunt for years and this pirate has uncovered quite a few gems. That diamond in the rough can be very deceiving and in some instances, it temporarily cost me my sanity. However, there's nothing greater than the ability to feel deeply about something or someone.

Society will criticize whether you stay in a loveless marriage with no mutual respect, or seek a respectable counterpart with a side order of passion. I always knew there was no sadder thought than opening my front door ten years later still feeling dead inside. My sadness pushed me to take a risk and not be the dutiful girl who plays it safe; I've always played it safe for fear I'd be judged. My inner soul burned for passion and I found it, though short-lived. The prospect of being touched so deeply was always worth the risk of being alone. How exhilarating to be standing on top of that mountain with the hope of being blown away?

I often wonder if my choices influenced my children and how it translated to their view of the world. I am perfectly imperfect but my life is lived honorably with great self-respect as a mother and a person. It took years for me to realize that living an honorable life means giving myself the wonderful gift of me, because no one will ever love me more than I am capable of loving myself. Perhaps focusing on self-respect has been the greatest choice of all, but at the end of the day my nemesis is Father Time. There's much to celebrate daily although I temporarily fall into that zone of *wanting more than what I have.*

While battling that negative thought on a long-distance phone call, my close friend Dane asked me the question, "Can you imagine asking God for more than what you already have?"

I paused to think about that question.

My parents, tipping the scale closer to ninety, both still exceedingly healthy, have witnessed the birth of their first great grandchild. Often I become upset with myself when I'm impatient with their slow verbal response time or hearing them recite stories that I've heard multiple times, sometimes within the same visit. My impatience has underlying anger, but not with them. It stems from wanting their aging process to slow down and not take its natural course of pulling them closer to the end of their lifeline. I cannot imagine my world without them.

My mother phoned my grandmother every morning, way back when. I call my mother every morning, and Sadie calls both of us on her way to her work. It's tradition. Time will eventually steal my mother from us, and Sadie and I will unconsciously make that call to her with no answer on the other end. We'll laugh and cry to each other at the same time and talk about how the heavens snatched the best of the best. Eerily, my phone holds several of my parents' voice messages, stored for the future so I can remember the sound of their voices.

I've become the strongest of us, my parents, that is. On many levels that makes me uncomfortable. I'm conflicted with sorrow and guilt. They have been my lifeline, my emotional rock with whom I've shared my struggles, but they have reached a plateau where sharing conversations that can shake their world in a negative way must be considered. I have learned to be my own pillar of strength with the confidence that I can carry the weight of the world on my shoulders.

The years have left me unscathed by tragedies that I've seen others battle through. Sadie and Jack, raised in a fragmented home, have flourished into healthy, educated, successful, and engaging adults. They're my magnificent offspring equipped with a good moral compass that I often compare to others who were raised in intact families. I'm warmed inside and out by the mere thought of them and it's a fuzzy feeling. This is the only time I smile, with a foolish giggle, and truly don't give a shit how many lines appear on my face. My world glows in anticipation of their visits. When I randomly remind them about some asinine antics that took place when we lived together years ago it's not to be annoying, but my mode of remembering that moment in time when life seemed simpler; a time in my life so well-defined. This is where the garden comes into play. My garden is now their garden to visit and I trust they're growing their own with the tools they've been given.

Jack doesn't realize that when we're together he creates new memories for me that will replace the ones I may forget. When Jack was working full-time and attending graduate classes, he would visit with me for dinner one night during the week. I recall a particular Wednesday, Jack arriving just past six o'clock in the evening. and immediately changing into workout clothes that I store for him in a basket. The gym is something we enjoy together. It was admirable to watch him push through the exhaustion and his face was sweeter than ever! Riding the elevator, I'd stare at him with pride, hoping that others would ride our elevator car, too. My face beamed when I introduced him; similar to when he was an infant and I would pull back the crocheted baby blanket in his carriage to put him on display.

After an abbreviated workout we returned to the apartment. He relaxed on the couch enjoying a bowl of red grapes while I prepared a special dinner with extras for him to take home. The conversation was minimal because he was completing assignments on his laptop while eating his meal, but he was apologetic.

Our car ride back to his apartment after that midweek dinner is indelible. As soon as he crawled into the passenger seat I knew that the movement of the ride would encourage him to close his eyes. In those quiet moments I wanted to engage him in conversation but held back. Country music played softly, and he knew the song well.

Jack took my hand in his and said, "Listen to the words of

this song with me and tell me if you like it."

He lifted the top of my hand to his lips and said, "I love my mommy."

When I glanced over to say, "I adore you, my son," sleep had taken him away.

Jack, from time to time, can get into an overly endearing mood with me, which carries me to a place that words cannot describe. My relationships with both Jack and Sadie are close and their presence in my life moves me. I continue to embrace my seriousness of purpose as their mother. They have cultivated lives of their own and my alone time with them is less frequent, but more cherished.

Sadie married well. She and her husband have made Manhattan their home and they are nurturing their own garden. I look up to the heavens and say, "Dear God, may she plant them better than I did," a thought I'll never share with her. I'm hesitant to bring her my seeds because some did not grow perfectly and fear being turned away with my small pouch. She and Jack are the best of my crop. At a comfortable distance I watch her plant her garden. She's smart and wise, and "gets it." I can now learn from her because I respect the road she's traveling. How ironic, I raised her. Sadie is a mature woman, an equal to me in thoughts and words, and I hope she finds life's most wonderful gifts along that road.

The streets of the city are bustling with the beginning of springtime. The view of the East River from my terrace is calming, and with a sigh of contentment I take another sip of my French pressed coffee with a touch of whipped cream. It's both amusing and disappointing to observe the pedestrians crossing the street, so unaware of one another. Their cell phones are the deterrent that prevents them from connecting to their surroundings, and so they miss out on life at that very moment. The text or the call *is* the moment and I suppose we are all creatures of habit.

I've settled into a wonderfully satisfying lifestyle with more blessings than I know what to do with. There's still a chill in the air, but I welcome the sunshine since the harsh winter has had its way with me.

A tap on my shoulder breaks my concentration and I stretch back my arm so Wes can hold my hand. Wes, another blessing. My hair is in a bun and I'm feeling like the old-fashioned 1950s girl. That thought makes me grin from ear to ear. Throughout my life I've wanted to emulate the women of that era, when roles and expectations were well-defined.

"I love those sexy lines around your mouth, Seppie."

I have changed slightly from year to year, but with both the beauty of wisdom and physical age.

He bends down to kiss me and that kiss always feels right. He feels right, but most important, I feel right. With all of my searching, the most important thing I discovered was the key to the chains that constrained me. I always held the key.

"I love you, Wesley Harlowe."

The sounds of waves ripple through my phone; Sadie's call is coming in.

"Hey, Sadie."

"Sep, can you come and meet me?"

There's a sense of urgency.

"I'm at Leaf and Bean Café."

"What's happening, Sadie, you sound frantic?"

It's always a mother's worry that her child and grandchild are not okay, but her breathing slowed and her words are intelligible so I'm more at ease. She believes that I am her magician who has all of the answers, so I pretend that I am her magician and dear God, I love her more than ever.

"Okay, Sadie, I need a little bit of time to put on jeans and a sweater. What is this about?"

"Just come, Sep," she says curtly.

I dress quickly and pull on my green suede boots that we purchased together.

"Wes, I'll be back within an hour or two. Going to meet Sadie. I'm not sure what's going on."

"Is she okay?"

"No details, but if there's any concern, I'll call you. Love you."

"Love you, too."

My concierge hails a cab for me and though this is an impromptu meetup with Sadie, it's always a treat to be with her.

After sitting in a substantial amount of traffic to make it over to the West Side, I hop out of the cab. Leaf and Bean Café is half a block away and my eyes scan the street for the red baby carriage. A red baby carriage certainly makes a statement! One day I would like Sadie to paint a black-and-white picture of her with the baby carriage amid the scenery of the city streets; only the carriage in sepia.

As I approach Leaf and Bean Café there is a long wait to be seated and I place myself at the end of the line to leave my name. This pricey café is not my favorite, but Sadie enjoys their organic salads and the spaciousness inside can accommodate carriages and strollers.

Just a few minutes pass and Sadie makes her way toward me from the back of the restaurant.

"Where is the baby?" I ask in a hurried voice. "You're with Elle, yes?'

"Of course, Sep, I'm with Elle. I have a good spot in the back with her carriage."

I must laugh because Sadie has always called me by my first name and the reactions of others are so varied. Some have voiced that she is showing disrespect, but in my heart I recognize it is truly her display of endearment. Fuck the critics!

Concerned about Elle being left unattended I follow Sadie to the back of the café, my hobo bag slamming into everyone's chair along the way. Fuck them, too. We're on a mission to get seated. At our table, a young girl is seated beside the red carriage and Sadie didn't tell me she would be inviting a friend to join us.

I unbutton my jacket, as I approach the table, and unwind my scarf until I stop dead in my tracks. My face becomes ashen and my body freezes.

I'm looking down at Lily.

CHAPTER 18

Reconnecting with Lily

A steady stream of flashbacks and intense emotions rented every available space in my head. Lily looks different from the pictures I've kept in my phone. Her body filled out beautifully—she became a woman. Her lush head of hair remains the same and I can still imagine my fingers sifting through each strand when I would brush before she left for school. Eight years ago, I sat on the front lawn of her house, looking up at her bedroom window knowing I couldn't see her again. There are so many questions to ask her and things I want to share, all the while I'm watching the entrance to the Leaf and Bean Café for fear that Teddy will appear and drag her away.

"Sadie," I asked, "How did this happen? How...?"

"I was out shopping with Elle, and Lily and I walked past each other on the street. Both of us instantly turned around and voilà! She's beautiful, isn't she? Lily is a third-year student at Columbia studying pre-law.

"Thank you for saying that, Sadie," Lily replied, "and thank you for inviting me to sit with you for coffee. How wonderful it is that you're a mother now with a precious little girl. She's a cutie pie."

I cannot believe I'm hearing Lily's voice.

"Lily, you are as beautiful as ever and a blessing that you and Sadie found each other this afternoon. Not a day went by that I haven't thought about you, and now you're in college!"

I looked at Sadie and knowing that she reads me well, she knows that I want to address the elephant in the room.

"How is your dad these days, Lily? I hope he is well?"

As the question dropped out of my mouth, my body stiffened and I braced myself to hear that he remarried and happiness filled their home the way I thought that I once would.

"Sep," Sadie said, "I need to get going with Elle. Josh will be home early from the office and I must get to the market before dinner, but the two of you should continue your conversation. Lily and I had a chance to catch up and she's finished with her afternoon classes."

"Of course, Sadie. Lily, are you okay with spending some time with me?" My eyes are still wandering toward the entrance for Teddy's possible appearance.

In the back of my mind Lily is still Teddy's underage child and it's hard to shake this guilty feeling that I'm engaging with his daughter.

"I'm totally good on time, Seppie. That's why I asked Sadie to call you and have you meet us here."

Lily watched Sadie bundle up Elle in her carriage.

"Sadie, it was so great to see you and the baby. I hope we will see each other again."

"Likewise, Lily," Sadie responded with a smile. "Today was

absolutely an unexpected treat for both me and Sep."

Lily giggled.

"Sadie, I always got a kick out of the fact that you called your mom by her first name."

Both my girls giggled and I wanted to cry.

There's a lineage that flows from my mother to me, to Sadie, and now to Elle. Generations of strong, remarkable women so deeply connected and our little Elle will join our ranks. Our family is blessed. Where is Lily's lineage? She barely knew her mother and was extricated from me without a moment's notice. The assumption that Teddy has remarried and a new family has formed for Lily is the only bittersweet silver lining that will bring some peace to the pain we endured. Likely her stepmother has children of her own and with great hope she has treated Lily like a daughter, providing her with a sense of family among her own children.

My life has both passion and stability with a solid, noble man worthy of my affection. He and I bring out the best parts of each other, and there is no white noise that disturbs our peace. When I look at Wes I see myself in his eyes and our intimacy breathes life into each other. That being said, I also had a life before Wes and loved Teddy so profoundly. I refuse to believe that it's a sin to carry some of that emotion as a souvenir for which I've traveled far. I've earned the luxury of not suppressing my thoughts as long as it doesn't weigh me down or unbalance my scale. At this moment Lily's presence makes me feel very much alive, but it draws in her father's ghost from the shadows. Perhaps the scale has tipped just a tiny bit?

Lily stood up and gave Sadie a tight hug, then kissed her finger and pressed it on Elle's forehead.

"Bye-bye, baby Elle. See you soon."

Sadie gave me a kiss, then left the café, leaving me with Lily.

"So, Lily...ahhh...where do we even begin?" I said not knowing how to segue again to the question about Teddy. "As you can see so much has transpired since I saw you. Sadie is married and now has Elle. Jack became a veterinarian and is working in Midtown. His dream to open his own clinic will take some time. And you, my dear, are planning on becoming an attorney and following in your dad's footsteps?"

"Yes," replied Lily. "Next summer I hope to secure an internship, hopefully in the city. I'm interested in environmental law."

"Are you in a dorm at Columbia or did you take an apartment with some friends? After the first year of college many students don't return to dorm life," I probed.

"Exactly, I dormed last year and met a pretty wonderful guy. He and I are both planning to sit for our LSATs, but are interested in different branches of law. We have so much in common and decided to share an off-campus apartment this year. You would like him. His name is Adam."

"Oh, I'm sure I would Lily. Is he from Connecticut, as well?"

"Actually, Adam is from the Midwest, but I've had an opportunity to visit his family with him during our last school break. Midwesterners are very down-to-earth people. Adam and I started out as best friends and it grew into a relationship. Pretty remarkable, isn't it?"

When I glanced again toward the front entrance, I saw a side view of a tall, assuming man walk in and my heart skipped a beat. The Leaf and Bean Café became crowded and now I'm having a flashback to when Teddy bumped into me at The Headless Horseman, knocking over my drink. That first look was everything.

"It sure is, Lily, and a good foundation for a relationship."

"Adam has been my rock," she said looking down now. "We met in an on-campus bereavement group for students who have lost loved ones."

Typical Teddy. He should have had Lily in counseling when she first lost her mother. It's astounding to me that it has taken this long for poor Lily to find emotional support among other young adults who share her experience.

"Yes, Adam and I both lost our fathers a few months apart," she said, with her head still down, but eyes looking up at me.

I stared at her and then looked again for the man who was standing at the entrance, in total confusion about what she said. She should have said that Adam lost his father and she lost her mother. Lily has it all wrong and her words must have gotten jumbled, saying something different than what she intended.

"Lily, I'm relieved that you became part of a support group to share your feelings about your mom passing away. I always wanted that for you, but unfortunately I didn't have a voice to suggest it. I'm so sorry."

"Seppie," Lily reiterated, "I lost my father to Alzheimer's."

Nausea rolled around in my stomach and I worked hard to compose myself in front of Lily. Part of me wanted to cry for her and cry for me, but then anger took over. Teddy will never know the pain that he caused us. He'll never know that I loved him with every fiber of my being and that no woman could have endured his lunacy. If only I had the satisfaction of telling him that I figured out how perfectly he scripted my emotional sabotage while luring me in like a snake. His venom was both poisonous and addicting, and traces of it still run through my bloodstream.

"Skyline had suggested a bereavement group due to the severity of Dad's condition," Lily further explained. "Skyline is an assisted living facility on the Upper West Side and Dad was moved there this past year. He was diagnosed during my senior year of high school and not long after, we hired full-time help at the house. The progression of the disease was unpredictably fast. Now he barely recognizes me. It's sad to visit there, and Adam has been very helpful. It seems easier to make peace with Dad's illness in a bereavement group. The support group for children of parents with Alzheimer's was not a good fit for me. I've been spending weekends in Greenwich cleaning out the house in preparation for placing it on the market. The practical choice is to sell because Dad will never return to it and I can't manage a big house. Seppie, I know this comes as a shock."

"I don't know what to say." My words trickled out unintelligibly. "I can only imagine that it is heartbreaking to see Dad's mind separate from his body. Lily, you've been through a private war and if there's any way that I can help, you know that I will do anything for you. Since you were very young when I left, legally we could not have maintained a relationship unless Dad had agreed to it."

As I spoke, my words were pouring out.

"I know that, Seppie, and I was always aware that Dad smothered our relationship. My last memory was of you sitting outside on the lawn. I was frightened when I was sent to my room. I shut the light, kneeled down by the window, and fell asleep crying."

"I looked up, Lily, I looked up," I cried, losing composure and giving in to my emotions. "I looked up, I looked up, dear

God, I looked up."

Lily knelt down by my chair, hugged me, and said, "You will never lose me again. I saved remembrances of you after that night. I kept a box under my bed with all the special things that you gave me. Each day I added some of your favorite pieces of clothing to the box, from Dad's closet, in fear that he would throw away everything. When I went to sleep, I felt you in the room."

My eyes dried in the fabric of Lily's sweater and I could smell her favorite vanilla fragrance from L'Occitane. "I have a question about something that only you can answer," Lily continued.

"Of course, honey," I said, holding both her hands as she returned to her chair.

"I'm going through Dad's personal financial documents and I came across his credit card statements. He was fanatical about saving hard copies of his statements in his filing cabinet. Do you remember when you and Dad would go to that hotel in the city every year? The Beaumont?"

"Yes, of course. Why?"

"Well, it's confusing as to why Dad would have booked two hotel rooms on the nights that you went together. Didn't you and Dad stay in the same room?"

I'm dumbstruck!

"Yes, Lily. We were always together in the room. It could have been the hotel's error that they double charged. I'm sure that's what it was."

"I don't think it was an error. It wasn't an error on just one statement. The charge for two rooms appeared each year that both of you stayed there. Adam called the hotel with Dad's account number and they confirmed that two suites were reserved, separate floors, one above the other. Did he invite other people to stay at the hotel on those evenings?"

"No, Lily, certainly not that I'm aware of. That's strange, no?"

"Yes, very strange."

I recall rushing to The Headless Horseman looking for Teddy on the night of Lily's frantic phone call and opening the door to the empty Blue Room. Holy shit, could it be that he had me in the hotel room while he was having sex with someone else one floor below? None of this makes sense, and when I think that I couldn't be more bottomed out from a relationship, this is crushing. Why did he bring me there? He could have had sex at the hotel on a night he'd say that he's working late.

"Lily, now that I'm thinking about it, you're right. Each year he treated his partner and his wife to a night at the hotel. Dad was always very generous in that regard. Silly me. I can't believe I forgot about that, but it has been a long time."

The last thing I'd want to do is cause Lily more anguish.

"Okay. Well, that's the missing piece to the puzzle," Lily said with a sigh of relief. "I apologize if it hurt you to bring this up."

"No worries. I'm glad we cleared that up. We expended a lot of emotional energy this past hour. Oh my goodness, an hour and a half, Lily!" I checked my watch.

"It feels so good to be with you, Seppie."

"Can I expect that we'll stay in touch? Of course, that's up to you and how comfortable you feel. I've missed you, Sweet Pea."

"Sweet Pea? Oh my," Lily said in a little girl's voice, "You used to put me to bed and call me Sweet Pea." She wrapped her arms around me. "Yes, yes. We have years of catching up and I want you to meet Adam. Can you put my number and address in your phone?"

"I will do that right now," I said as I flipped through my contacts. Lily's contact is still under Sweet Pea, as Teddy agreed to buy her a phone just a few months before I left the house. I never deleted her.

"Should I change the contact to read as Lily?" I asked as I showed her my phone.

"No, please don't. That would show an interruption in our lives."

CHAPTER 19

Lily and I Continue

No sooner did I reach my apartment, Sadie calls.

"Sep, how did things go with Lily?"

"Sadie," I said with exasperation, "Did you know? Did you know...about Teddy?"

"Of course, I knew," she replied quickly. "That was one of the first questions that I asked, but now I'm worried about you."

"Worried about me? Nonsense. There's no need to worry about me. It was very emotional to see Lily all grown-up but are you okay?"

"Why would I not be okay?" questioned Sadie.

"Well, you and I are joined at the hip and if Lily is reintroduced into our lives I want to be sure that you're okay with that. I'm almost certain that your brother would be fine, as would Wes. Wes also knows about Lily and, with Teddy's condition, it would not pose a threat. I feel for her and want to be able to offer her support."

"As you should," encouraged Sadie. "All of us really liked Lily and it isn't her fault that her father is the devil incarnate, a wolf in sheep's clothing, or whatever the hell you want to call him."

"Wow. Okay, that's extreme."

"Sep, I speak my mind. If it's on the lung, it's on the tongue," she said with conviction. "I bullshit you not. After all, I'm my mother's daughter."

"You sure are. Well, I would like to have her over and she would like me to meet Adam. How would you feel about joining us, with Josh of course? I can make a nice dinner and I'm sure that Wes would be on board."

"That sounds fine, but don't you think you're jumping the gun? It might be best to have Lily spend some alone time with you so she's not overwhelmed. Though she would love for you to meet Adam, she likely mentioned it very matter-of-factly, as let's *consider doing this in the near future* kinda thing. Seeing her again is a shock to your system in addition to her no longer having a mother or a father. Be very sure that you want to re-engage. When you were living with her, she had a father and you were a support. The way it looks now you're the whole kit and caboodle and this has nothing to do with me. I'm good with whatever you decide."

Sadie, that little bitch. I adore her beyond, beyond, beyond. It kills me that she knows me so well. She knows what's right, and she always sees situations clearly and objectively. If I try to back away from her advice and put blinders on, she'll tell me that I raised her right and not to complain.

Less than an hour later Wes came home and we discussed my day's events during dinner. Wes is a good listener and knows how to ask all the right questions in a loving and non-judgmental way. He allows me the freedom to arrive at my own conclusions without criticism. Though divorced with no children of his own, he cares for mine and follows my lead. One of his greatest moments was Elle's birth, making him feel like a grandpa though we're not married. He's receptive and ready to open the door for Lily's entrance.

Later that night I had difficulty falling asleep though Wes held me close to him. He could sense my restlessness because we sleep with our bodies entwined. Images of Teddy were scrambling around in my head and I was feeling both sad and angry. If he were dead, it would be easy to resolve the many questions that are biting at me. Is there a significant other who visits him, a wife or girlfriend? And every time he made love to the woman who succeeded me was each episode fiery and innovative because he couldn't remember what the fuck they did the night before? It's likely his Alzheimer's has removed any recollection of his deplorable behavior toward me and the poor bastard probably doesn't know which end is up. It would feel awkward to observe what was once a sexually appealing body, as he looks through me with his vacant eyes not remembering the agony he inflicted. God forgive me for having these thoughts. If he has a glimmer of memory, it might be a sweet one and then lights out and curtains down. Then again, all would be sweet because he had never taken one iota of responsibility for his actions, a legend in his own mind. The difference now is that I'm no longer trapped in his web and he's become the spider who will perish on the web that he has spun. Beautiful, beautiful Teddy. All tangled up with no place to go.

I waited a few days before calling Lily and lo and behold,

she beat me to the chase. I was delighted when Sweet Pea lit up my screen with a gaggle of geese soliciting me to answer. Lily always liked that ringtone and I never changed it.

"Lily," I answered. "It's so nice to hear from you. With all that's occupying your time I thought I would wait a bit before getting back in touch."

"I've been smiling since I bumped into Sadie and Elle, and having the chance to be with you again was a dream come true. Please say that you'll accept an invitation for lunch at my apartment. I'm working on a tight schedule between studying and cleaning out the Greenwich house on the weekends but would Sunday morning work? I'm thinking ten-thirtyish? Adam heads to the gym at that time and we could have our alone time. Say yes."

"Sunday would be perfect. Yes! If it makes it easier you can come to me, so you aren't fussing."

"Oh please, I won't hear of it," Lily argued. "You've been tremendous to me and I want to have you over. It will make me feel so good."

"Well, thank you. I would love to see your apartment. Expect that I'll bring some goodies and please, no argument there."

"Very well, no argument from me. You certainly know me well enough to know that I never turn down surprises."

The next few days were at a crawl. I was filled with anticipation trying to tailor my questions to Lily. When I tried to run some thoughts by Sadie, she said I should allow the conversation to flow naturally and enjoy the beauty of reconnecting.

"That's typical Sep," voiced Sadie. "Apply the screws the second you walk through her front door."

Double bitch. She's right again, indeed her mother's daughter. Sadie takes those liberties with me because she knows her shit and I sure did raise her right.

Sunday was an overcast day and I woke up extra early to buy a few things from Union Bay Market and Bakery. I brought down a sturdy wicker basket from the top of my closet and began filling it with special things that I know Lily loves. Pomegranate juice in that large impressive glass bottle, chocolate croissants, Linzer tortes, tangerines, and a bunch of purple tulips went into the basket. At ten-fifteen. I jumped in a cab and headed to her apartment with nervous excitement.

Lily and Adam's apartment is a three-floor walk-up close to Columbia University. The front of the building is in need of renovation, but a sweet little garden in the front enclosed by a flowery, wrought-iron fence gives it a homey look. I entered the lobby and rang up to their apartment. A buzzer clicked me in. The three-floor climb winded me, but my heart was already beating at a faster pace from my eagerness to see my Lily. At the top of the stairs, I regained composure and allowed my breathing to slow to normal. Their apartment, just to the right of the stairwell, welcomes visitors with a doormat that reads Every Day Is Hump Day for our Dog. Now that's funny! Teddy bought her Brownie, a cute dachshund when he was a puppy and I'm happy that the leasing agent allows pets. I pressed hard on the doorbell, but it didn't seem to be working so I knocked gently, wiping my feet on the mat.

"Welcome! Welcome to our home," said Adam as the door flung open. "I can't tell you enough how much of a pleasure it is to meet you. Please, come in!"

"Adam, the pleasure is all mine. You've got yourself the best girl in the world and from what I hear, she's found her lucky charm!"

Adam stands about five feet eleven inches and a bit on the husky side with a boyish look. His smile can light up a room.

Lily rushes to the door, looks into the basket, and cups both hands to her mouth.

"What have you done, Seppie?" she blurts out. "This is way too much!"

Coming closer she peels away some of the tissue paper and her eyes well up.

"Oh, oh my, all of my favorites. You remembered everything, and oh, the tulips! Where in the world did you find purple tulips?" she asked ecstatically.

"Seek, my love, and ye shall find."

"Let me take the basket from you, Seppie, so we can take your coat," Adam offers.

"Please do, and, Adam, thank you for the warmest welcome. It's really nice to be in your home. Love the doormat, by the way!"

I could smell the aroma of something sweet in the kitchen.

"Yes, we know. The doormat has become quite the conversation piece. Well, I'm going to rush out on both of you and hit up the gym. I need to keep my girlish figure," he teased, patting down his belly. "Lily will show you around and I hope we'll see each other soon. Don't be a stranger, here. Got it?" he said, as he wagged his finger at me.

"I sure do, boss. It will take wild horses to keep me away."

Adam opened his arms.

"Give me a hug before I leave," he playfully demanded.

I complied and moved in close to him. His hug is sincere and heartfelt. A woman knows these things. He picked up his gym bag by the front door and blew a kiss to Lily.

"See you later, Tiger Lily!"

Tiger Lily, I really like that. Lily found herself a delightful counterpart, and intuition tells me he's the right one for her. I wonder how well Teddy knows Adam and if he tried to work his magic to sabotage Lily's choice. From what I've heard and what I observe, he seems to be a stable young man raised well.

"Seppie, let me show you around. The apartment is not very big, but we've managed to make the most of our space."

I stepped into the apartment and Lily pointed to the little red doggie bed just outside the entrance to the kitchen.

"I think you remember Brownie? You knew him when he was a puppy."

Brownie jumped out of his velour bed and I picked him up, holding him close to me. With my nose buried in his fur the familiar scent of his shampoo reminded me of Teddy's bathroom after Brownie was bathed.

"You see, Seppie, he remembers you!"

Then very officially, as though she were a Realtor, "This is our functional, but cute, non-eat-in kitchen. Kinda small, but a substantial amount of cooking actually takes place here," she said convincingly. "I do have something special in the oven as we speak."

"Very impressive, Lily," now following her into the main living space. "And this is your living room and dining area. The colors are warm and inviting. Oh, and you have large picture windows that face the back of your building with a lot of greenery. This apartment is very special and a great find. I absolutely love it!"

"Excuse me for just a sec," apologized Lily, "I need to check on my masterpiece in the oven. Feel free to look around."

The small dining room table was set with bamboo placemats and I recognized the ivory ceramic plates from Teddy's house. Lily added lavender cotton napkins and set down vintage depression drinking glasses in a bluish-purple hue. It all seemed to work creatively. My assumption is that she is being selective with what to save and what to sell from their house.

While walking the short distance to the couch, my eyes were drawn to the oblong Scandinavian table behind it with pictures in mismatched frames. The pictures spanned from past to present of both Lily and Adam and their families. Everyone seems to be represented and looking closely, still holding Brownie in my arms, I notice a framed picture of Teddy, Lily, and me on a Thanksgiving morning when she was just a little girl. Beside that picture was another that Teddy had taken of me kneeling down to put on Lily's fur hat. Her eyes are looking up at me with an adorable pouty face. It's one of those random shots that if you tried to pose for it, you could never capture that moment.

"Seppie, lunch is just about ready," she called out from the kitchen breaking my concentration. I was warmed inside and out that through the years she has kept me close.

"I think you'll like what I've made."

"Can I help you with anything?" I called back.

"Absolutely not. Just sit down and relax and I will bring everything out."

Lily brought out a blueberry blintz soufflé that I used to make with her when we lived together. She rested the dish on a trivet.

"Voilà!" Lily sang. "Do you recognize this fabulous creation?"

"You bet I do! I didn't realize that you made note of all the ingredients that I used. How did you...?"

"Soon after you left, I knew if I didn't write down how you

prepared some of our special dishes, I would never remember it as a grown-up."

"Well, your dad was the chef of the house and we both know that his culinary skills surpassed mine. He would make the most fantastic meals with ingredients that I never even heard of."

"This blueberry blintz soufflé made from simple ingredients has always been my favorite," said Lily with a smile. "I remember on some Sunday mornings when Dad was still asleep you'd wake me up and ask me to help you prepare this to surprise him. Do you remember?"

"Yes, honey, I do."

Lily sauntered back to the kitchen and made two more trips to bring out the remainder of the food. She prepared an arugula and baby spinach salad with portabella mushrooms, shallots, and warm vinaigrette in a retro lavender glass bowl. Proudly she placed the pomegranate juice on the table next to a pitcher of her spiced iced tea.

"Oops, one more thing, don't move! "Lily hurried back in to the kitchen.

Returning to the table with a large mason jar filled with the purple tulips she shouted, "Mangia, mangia!"

This is the first time that I was able to enjoy Lily and feel comfortable speaking freely without fear of overstepping my bounds with Teddy.

"So, Lily, how often do you visit Dad at Skyline?"

"Well, I don't go as often as I should because he doesn't recognize me and it's so painful. Every once in a while he will ask me a question that is in the present, but when I answer him he looks at me as though I have four heads. It's pitiful. I am so sorry, Seppie, but you asked. I don't want to depress you, and I'm grateful that you will have me in your life after everything that Dad put you through. Don't ever think I was an oblivious kid."

I reached out and squeezed her hand.

Lily continued, "This entire process of juggling school, dealing with the house, and not to mention all the financials have taken a toll on me. Dad's accountant and financial advisors are being paid handsomely to walk me down this arduous path, consulting with the partners in Dad's firm. Adam is a sweetheart and sometimes I ask myself what I've done to deserve him, and now you're here. There really is a God. The medical professionals are unsure, day-to-day, about Dad's condition, but we do know he will never leave that facility. The disease has progressed and continues to advance quickly."

"Lily, is there anyone else who visits him aside from you and Adam, other family or friends? Maybe that would jog his memory. It's been such a long time since Dad and I were together. I would only presume that he found a special someone to enjoy spending time with."

A knot grew in my stomach from asking the one question that's been gnawing at me, not certain that I want to hear her reply.

Lily spoke slowly and guardedly.

"Not long after you left the house Dad brought someone new into our home. I became very rebellious, as you can well imagine, and I missed you terribly. She did move in with us and after a short time Dad surprised her with an engagement ring."

My heart sank as I dreamed of that moment when he would ask me to be his wife. Heaven knows I played that part to a tee, both with him and in loving Lily as a daughter. And so, he married another woman. I'm curious as to how she's managing his illness, the house, and every last detail. Does she have any claim to the house and has she actively taken responsibility as Lily's stepmother? Does she have children? My thoughts are overflowing and I'm working hard to think clearly.

"So, how is your relationship with your stepmom?"

"She's not my stepmom," Lily corrected me.

"You said that she and Dad..."

"She and Dad never married," Lily said firmly. "I would often hear them argue, mostly because Naomi would attack him with questions about his past relationships. Your name was mentioned quite a lot and so was my mom's. Dad would immediately shut down the conversation, being dismissive just like he was with you. Naomi was insistent that she needed to know the details of his past to move forward with marriage. Little did she know that Dad had a low threshold for being interrogated and their relationship would end in a flash."

"Many times I would skulk around when they were behind closed doors," she continued, "just to gather crumbs of information so I'd know what to expect. As their arguments increased so did the tension in our house, and when Dad didn't sleep upstairs Naomi would become short with me the following morning out of sheer frustration with my father.

"I will never forget the morning he asked her to pack her things. I was waiting for her to drive me to school. Naomi said she didn't give a shit if I was late for school and stayed in the kitchen to argue with Dad. Dad grabbed his jacket, ordered me to leave the house with him, and demanded that she pack up all of her things from the house by the end of the day. In desperation she bargained with him, even threatening to hurt herself if he didn't work things out with her. Sadly she couldn't convince him. Dad sent me to our next-door neighbor who drove me to school with her son. When I returned home that day, he said he had called a crisis team to remove her from our house. Dad prepared a royal dinner for the two of us and not another word was spoken about Naomi since."

"Lily, I am so sorry that you've carried these burdens. I promise you that I will stay in your life as long as you want me to. Also, and I'm not certain that I should say this to you, all those years that Dad and I went to the city for his firm's party, I never accompanied him to the Blue Room."

"That makes zero sense," Lily said in a confused tone.

"When I told you that Dad reserved that extra hotel room for his partner and his wife, I wasn't being honest. I didn't know about that additional room until you asked me about it. It actually makes me wonder if he was there with Naomi. Everything is running through my head right now, but one thing you must know is that the Blue Room was always off-limits to me. Dad wanted to keep his work separate from his personal life and oh, how I wanted to be a part of it; a part of everything. I dreamed about walking into that room with him, on his arm, for years. At one point the Blue Room became my obsession until I finally let it go. Dad was a very strong force and I conceded more than I fought with him. Most times I took his word as gospel because I truly wanted to make a loving home for all of us. There's so much more, but I want to move forward and not step back. You have a long road ahead of you and I want to comfort you in any way I can, be a source of support and not another worry."

Lily let out a long sigh and with a little bit of comic relief said, "The next time you come over, we should make this soufflé together, just like old times."

"Sweet Pea, how about you showing me how to make one of your special dishes."

Lily poured each of us some pomegranate juice and we raised our glasses for a toast.

"To new beginnings, Seppie. Our new beginning."

Clinking our glasses and taking a sip, made it official.

CHAPTER 20

Lily Joins Our Family

Lily and I embarked on our adventure of rekindling our relationship. I began to play a significant role in her life. It was easy to weave her into the fabric of the Webb family and she became an integral part of our lives. Lily wanted to emulate Sadie in many ways, and for the first time she experienced the comfort of a complete family. Adam jumped on board from day one and participates in all of the Webb holidays and special occasions, as he and Lily jockey between New York and his family in the Midwest. Both have rounded out our family circle.

It seems to be taking an enormous amount of time to clear everything from Teddy's house, and I feel guilty not offering my help. It would feel eerie to go back to the memories that breathe within the walls of that house. Much transpired under that roof; love, passion, hope, torment, despair, and the slow death of a dream. The flame burned within me for the longest time yearning to reach back to our beginning when I thought Teddy's love for me was genuine; it was a low and easy tide, the calm before the storm, I suppose. There's a part of Teddy that lives in me through Lily, as crazy as he was. I have reconciled that Teddy's feelings for me weren't real, and he was never capable of real love. All of the energy that he expended posturing left him depleted, too empty to explore the possibility of mutual respect and commitment.

Oh, if only I had ten minutes with a dead person it would be his late wife. Was she someone extraordinarily special whom no one can replace? Was she a simpleton and easy to govern? Teddy told me that Tessa died unexpectedly from a heart attack, a result of a diagnosed blood disorder called primary thrombocythemia, but when I delved sympathetically he refused to talk about it. He firmly said that he and Lily had suffered enough and insisted that I refrain from ever talking about it with his daughter. Life goes on, he would say.

Intimidated, I never mentioned Tessa, though I wondered if Lily knew that her mom suffered from a blood disorder. Teddy was a con man, a mad man, Spider-man, and I was hoodwinked by his lies, overwrought by his madness, caught in his web. Maybe God forced me to experience the worst of the worst to know when the best came along. I'm blessed now to love a man like Wes, solid and upright like my dad, who doesn't control or attempt to define me. The truth about Teddy and his illness has freed me. Should Teddy's disease, his inability to think clearly, serve as proper closure on this segment of my life? I wish no ill will on anyone, but I may be sent straight to hell for rationalizing that Teddy's punishment of Alzheimer's fits the crime.

Often, when driving home I take a detour and pass by Skyline. On occasion I'll pull into the circle and crane my neck to look up at a random window on the eleventh floor. He's in there, hidden away on a locked unit, an ironclad fortress, that secures its Alzheimer residents. The area is spacious and designed to curtail their residents' confusion, so I've read. The villain is still confined and confused even with Skyline's amenities. Teddy can no longer summon his words to castrate, manipulate, denigrate, and humiliate. The monster, now an empty shell, sits by his window in some catatonic state with no memory of the last time he hailed a cab to the Blue Room or rode the elevator to the suite below to fuck Naomi while I lay in the bed above them pining to be in the Blue Room. I'm sure there's no memory of picking up fancy pastries from an all-night bakery to tell me that a waiter from the Blue Room boxed them up.

Seemingly, Teddy's outings are now limited to Skyline's passionate workers who take their residents on NYC excursions to jog crumpled memories. I envision Teddy boarding the Skyline shuttle bus with the other lost cattle, a psychologist in tow, to a museum with hopes that a painting will remind him of a place or time. The thought makes me laugh and cry at the same time. Teddy, a broken man, temporarily shattered my spirit. That's the thing about trying to cut and paste people. Regardless of where I wanted Teddy to be in my life, he always put me back where he thought I belonged...and now he's in a place harming no one.

Taking one last look at the eleventh floor, I shake my head in disillusionment before pulling away from the curb to make my journey home.

Lily and Adam both applied and were accepted to Brooklyn Law School. I'm certain that their road ahead will be fruitful and they will travel it together. When I speak of my children, I include Lily and Adam, who have brought another level of dimension to our family. They want to be with us. Lily and Adam, two beautiful and exceptional people. My bitterness about Teddy is curbed and I ask Lily about him only in a kind-hearted way. So many questions have gone unanswered, for Lily, too, I presume.

The remains in the Zezza house are dwindling in a conscious effort to clear out all of the rooms. Once the house is vacant it will be ready for the real estate market, and springtime is just around the corner. Lily placed most of the furniture on consignment and the household items that hold little or no meaning for her were donated to Habitat for Humanity.

The temperature has become frigid and most days are in the single digits. Today is Sunday and it's Valentine's Day—no secret that it's my most treasured day of the year. Wes has been preparing for our romantic dinner at home with all the accoutrements. As silly as he thinks Valentine's Day is, he shows his romantic side by appealing to my wishes and leaves no stone unturned. Shrimp and scallops over couscous with a side of asparagus are on the menu with a chickpea and kale salad to start. When I peeked into the fridge there was a paper bag on the bottom shelf, and he was chilling a bottle of my favorite sauvignon blanc, New Zealand, of course. Next to the bottle I noticed an unfamiliar plastic bag, and of course I took a peek. Inside is a plastic box with a red rose corsage. How sweet is that? I feel as though I journeyed far to be in this place of contentment.

The day is uncomplicated and Wes is happiest just to see me smile. We will be curling up on the couch to watch old movies and live in our moment. My children know how much

I adore Valentine's Day and I mailed everyone a card, a Seppie tradition. Disappointingly, no one called to thank me for the card or to wish me a Happy Valentine's Day. Maybe I am too over-the-top about Valentine's Day.

As six o'clock rolls around Wes is banging around the pots and pans and it's a welcome symphony. He is far from being a chef but whatever he prepares and however it turns out will be gourmet, as far as I'm concerned.

"Dinner will be ready in half an hour, Sep," Wes calls from the kitchen.

Minutes later he brings me the red rose corsage and I act surprised. Truly elated, I outstretch my arm for him to place it on my wrist.

"Oh my dear, sweet Wes, thank you. The corsage is beautiful and special, and I love you!"

I'm feeling very much like a schoolgirl going to my senior prom, and the pride and sparkle in his eyes makes me teary. It's not the expensive box of long-stemmed roses that cost $150 with no true meaning behind the purchase, but a wristlet with two roses that exemplify the unity of a man and a woman.

"I'm so glad that you like it, Seppie. Enjoy wearing it on Valentine's Day."

His sincerity is a rare find in most men nowadays, but Wes has that certain "somethin' somethin'." During dinner he periodically picks up my hand to smell the roses and kisses my hand softly. We are both proud of his efforts.

"Wes, I don't think I could love you more than I do right now. Thank you for being such a love in so many ways."

"Well," he touted, "the magic of Valentine's Day is not over!"

"Hmmm," I responded in a devilish voice, "more to come?

No way! Aha, I know what it is."

"September Webb, get that mind of yours out of the gutter!"

We laughed and both stood up to give each other a tight hug.

"Let me help with the cleanup," I offered.

"No argument here. I know that's your forte. We also have to make room for dessert."

"Dessert, too?"

While clearing the dishes and loading the dishwasher the intercom buzzes.

"Can you see who that is, Wes? My hands are wet."

"Sorry, Sep, I can't get to the door. Can you please answer it?"

Quickly wiping my hands on the dish towel I rush to the intercom.

"Yes?", holding down the button.

"Hello, September, it's Colton. There's a delivery for you and I'm sending someone up."

"Of course, thank you."

I went to find Wes and told him that a delivery was on its way up to our apartment.

"Oh, did you order something?" he asked. "I think I hear the doorbell."

Both of us open the door and six beautiful faces were standing in front of us. Lily and Adam brought boxes of desserts, Sadie undoubtedly made her fruit salad, and Josh was holding precious Elle. Jack, the last to walk in, handed me a card.

"That's my special surprise, Seppie," Wes said. "Today would not be complete unless we ended Valentine's Day as a family."

Each of my magnificent children entered the apartment with a hug for both Wes and me.

Sadie whispered in my ear, "Sep, this is what it means to have a man really love you."

The children stayed just over an hour because tomorrow is a workday, but nonetheless the evening was enchanting. Sadie and Lily quickly cleaned up like two busy bees while I had cuddle time with Elle. Could the day have been more perfect? Before leaving, Wes corralled everyone to huddle together for a picture and for the second picture squeezed in for a selfie with the family.

Happily exhausted, he and I retired for the night. When I came to bed, he had the corsage sitting on my pillow.

"Wes, can you put the corsage back on my wrist?"

He grinned from ear to ear.

"Wait," as he lifted his phone from the nightstand. He showed me the picture of all of us.

"This is our family, our beautiful family," then kissed me. "Now hold out your wrist."

He closed the lights and we embraced each other, as well as the peacefulness in our lives. My arm hung over his waist, careful not to crush the roses.

At 5:41 the honking of geese sounded on my phone. Startled, I thought it was my alarm then realized it is Lily's ringtone.

"Hi Lily, what's going on? Is everything alright?"

"Seppie, I am so sorry to call you this early. I just got a call from Skyline."

"Oh, no problem. Wes and I will be getting up soon anyway. Is everything okay with your father?"

"Actually, no. They called to tell me his symptoms have worsened. His breathing pattern has changed to a rapid, shallow panting and he is refusing food and liquids. They explained that in this stage of Alzheimer's the muscles in the throat weaken and it can be difficult to swallow. Seppie, I'm scared. I've read about this and when mucus accumulates to make this rattling sound they call it the 'death rattle.' Seppie, he's going to die soon. I don't want to hear that sound when I go to see him."

"I know, honey. What else did they say? Are they asking you to come to Skyline right away?"

"Well," Lily continued, "they also said that he is losing control of his bowel and urinary functions. I think I mentioned to you that he was diagnosed a little less than four years ago and moving through the stages very quickly. I need to get to Skyline after my two back-to-back morning classes."

"Okay, Lily," I said calmly, "I'm here for you. Will Adam be going with you? You can call me after your visit or I can meet you at Skyline. Let me know."

"Adam will not be going with me. I haven't visited Dad in a while and I need to go alone, but I'll be in touch with you afterward, Seppie. Thank you and I love you."

"Love you, too, pea. I'll wait to hear from you."

"Everything okay?" asked Wes, still half-asleep.

"Lily just got a call from Skyline. It sounds like Teddy is in his final stages. She's headed there today and sounds pretty frightened."

"Should you go with her?"

"No, I don't think so. She wants to go alone and make up for the time that she hasn't been visiting with him. You're a sweetheart for suggesting it, though."

I crawled in closer to Wes and found my niche under his arm. He kissed me on the top of my head and I closed my eyes.

CHAPTER 21

Death Approaches Teddy

Wes left the apartment at seven forty-five and I busied myself for most of the morning. The public schools are on mid winter break, therefore, I have a reprieve. I was focused on laundry and cleaning the apartment, but when eleven-thirty. rolled around I became anxious and preoccupied with checking my phone. Lily should be on her way over to Skyline and I was worried about her. Both my parents are still alive and Lily is about to lose her second parent. Am I being selfish not showing up to be with her, though she wants her privacy to spend his final days alone with him? Will she be okay to handle Teddy's rapidly declining condition? I paced the apartment until early afternoon then decided to send Lily a text message.

Today 1:17 p.m.
Lily, honey, I'm thinking about you.
Please text me to let me know you're okay.

Today 2:38 p.m.

Sorry, Seppie. Just saw your message

Dad is mostly unresponsive and I've been sitting here holding his hand.

His body feels cold, but docs say it's because at this stage of the disease the circulation is poor.

Today 2:39 p.m.

Sending hugs and prayers.

Call me if you'd like.

Today 2:40 p.m.

Thanks. Staying a little longer.

At a quarter to four Lily called and told me she was leaving Skyline and heading home.

"Seppie, it was really scary to see Dad in that state," Lily whimpered as she choked on her words. "So sad and pathetic. He has withered away. Adam is coming home soon. I should be okay."

"Okay, I'll check in with you later if I don't hear from you again. All of us are here for you."

As I hung up the phone I contemplated going to Skyline with Lily on her next visit. I've educated myself on Alzheimer's and from Lily's description it sounds as though Teddy is close to the end. The altruism in me whispers that going with Lily is the right thing to do.

The indecisiveness to go with Lily is emotionally holding me hostage and I feel disoriented. There are two overwhelming thoughts: Lily's response when I suggest visiting her dad with her at Skyline and, should we visit together, containing my reaction to seeing Teddy.

Settling in on my sofa, I close my eyes and imagine walking through the front doors of the fortress. My bags are checked for sharp objects, but all that's found is a box of poisonous pastries from that all-night bakery for the son of a bitch to choke on. I'm dozing off between heinous thoughts and in one snooze I dream that when I enter Teddy's room, he is elated to see me again. He looks exactly as I remember, then right before my eyes his entire being transforms into an ugly, spine-chilling creature from Chiller Theatre.

What am I doing to myself? I am planning to go.

Relieved that I've made a decision, it now seems less haunting. I believe I'll get the proper closure, especially because Lily is in my life again. I'll share this revelation with Wes to be certain that he's comfortable with my choice to visit.

Should I wear something from my wardrobe that Teddy might remember? The unforgiving side of me wants to flaunt what I still have in front of that twisted bastard. My dressing in all black can subtly send the message that his shadow of death is approaching in leaps and bounds and people receive what they put forth in life.

I must have fallen asleep because Lily's ringtone startled me. It's 6:19 p.m.

"Hey, Lily," I answered in a confused and sleepy voice. "I fell asl..."

"Dad just passed."

Her voice is monotone.

Sitting up, I tried to shake off the sleep.

"Oh my, oh my. Lily, I'm so sorry."

"Adam and I are headed over to Skyline to discuss funeral arrangements. I also need to put in a call to his trust and estate attorney and make a few other calls before I leave."

Lily was in shock and it was evident in her tone.

"Pea, what can I do to help you? Anything?"

"Can you come with me tomorrow morning to buy his casket? Sorry, Seppie. I never expected this would be so sudden. Adam can be with me in the afternoon, but I need to do this tomorrow morning."

"Of course, I'll go with you. Would you like me to go with both of you to Skyline now?"

"Thank you, Seppie, but we're good. Thank you for all that you do."

She hung up the phone. I sat in disbelief and cried. At this moment nothing makes sense. Random thoughts swirled around in my head as I began to make phone calls to deliver the news to my family, like the town crier.

Hear Ye, Hear Ye!

The Grim Reaper abducted one of our village's most evil and now everyone is safe.

I called Wes and he answered on the second ring.

"Hi, sweetheart, what's up?"

"Teddy passed. Lily just called. She and Adam are on their way over to Skyline. She asked me to go with her to buy his casket tomorrow morning. All other arrangements will be made this evening and the wake will likely be on Thursday."

"I'm so sorry, and how are you? How are you, really?"

"I have to be strong for Lily, she lost both of her parents and—"

"Stop, Seppie. How are you?"

"On one hand I'm sad for her loss, and on the other hand I'm really grateful that I can share this with you and we're both comfortable."

"You have me and your children, and Lily has all of us," Wes reassured me. "We will support each other as a family. I'll come home now."

Wes arrived home shortly after seven and I had time to jump in the shower and make myself presentable.

Who will attend the wake to pay their respects? How will I introduce myself? I've attended numerous wakes and the family usually stands in the front of the parlor while each attendee gives the family members a hug and offers their condolences. I am Lily's family, so should I stand next to her to receive the guests? Will Wes attend the wake with me? Should Sadie, Jack, and Josh attend with us? Is Adam's family planning to fly in from Milwaukee for the funeral?

I suppose I could speak to Lily about these things tomorrow while en route to Connecticut. Teddy will be buried in Fairfield County in Fair Gardens Cemetery next to Tessa. From what Teddy had shared when we were together, Lily has not visited the cemetery since her mother's death. Teddy had strong feelings about Lily moving forward and not upsetting her with visits to her mother's grave. This never made any sense to me, but Lily is not my child.

Should I help Lily explore her feelings about seeing her mother's grave after all of this time? She and I will have only a few hours together tomorrow morning, as she and Adam must make arrangements for funeral transportation, order memorial cards, prepare Teddy's burial suit, and compose the obituary.

Wes and I discussed, as a couple, what both of us would be comfortable with. I wanted to be certain that Wes wasn't agreeing to things, on my behalf, that he wouldn't be at ease with. He was open to being a support for us throughout the process and if Lily became overwhelmed, would step back.

I Googled the exact location of the cemetery and began making a short list of nearby restaurants where we could reserve a space for after the interment. Wes and I thought it best to make a reservation at a place that could provide us with a separate dining area accommodating fifteen to twenty people, not knowing if Adam's family would be joining us. This was the least we could do to take some weight off Lily and give her the option to cancel should she decide otherwise. After calling four restaurants we made a reservation at Josie and Her Sisters, a family-owned café offering a varied menu and a small private back room. The website photos look cheery and I would not choose a place that was dreary and dark. The maître d' was amenable to holding the reservation and allowing us to firm up the exact time by Wednesday at noontime.

Lily called late at night and asked if I could pick her up at eight forty-five the following morning. She had scheduled an appointment for nine forty-five at Fairleigh Funeral Home to select the casket and also bring any picture collage that she'd like displayed at the wake. Our conversation was under two minutes.

"Love you, Seppie. We'll talk more when I see you and thank you for doing this with me."

"Of course, Lily. Anything, anytime. Get some sleep."

At seven o'clock I was up and getting ready for the day. Wes and I had coffee together, then he left for work. I left the apartment shortly after eight, stopped at the corner Starbucks to pick up a large coffee and croissant for Lily, and then drove to her apartment.

"Good morning, Lily. I'm here. I'm waiting across the street in the car, whenever you're ready."

"Okay," she responded, sounding out of breath. "I'll be down in a few. Just getting the paperwork together."

I watched for her front door to open and finally Lily appeared. She was dressed in her white down jacket and carrying her gray-and-black fabric tote bag. Giving me a wave, I watched her cross the street.

"Hey, thank you, thank you for taking me to Connecticut today."

"Here," I said, giving her the Starbucks bag. "This is for you. Not sure if you had your coffee or breakfast this morning. I made a quick stop before coming here."

"It smells amazing, thank you! It was tough to get out of bed this morning. I couldn't fall asleep until three o'clock with all of my tossing and turning. I'll try not to fall asleep while you're driving."

"Not to worry, I'll put the address in the GPS and you can lay back and rest. Don't worry if you doze."

Lily read me the address from her phone and I programmed the GPS. It showed 9:37 as the estimated time of arrival. She sipped her coffee and ate the croissant as we drove peacefully, with little conversation.

"Seppie," Lily began. "I know today will be just as difficult for you as it will be for me. I'm hoping, if you're up to it of course, that you will come to the wake and the funeral. Am I asking too much of you?"

"No, pea, of course not. I spoke with Wes, Sadie, and Jack and all of us will be there with you, if you want us to. It's your call."

"Please, yes, it would mean so much to me," Lily responded with a sigh of relief.

"Likely Josh will stay with Elle, but the rest of us will be with you. Will Adam's family be flying in from Milwaukee?"

"His mom is planning a trip to New York during Easter and will stay for a few days. It's difficult for her to fly here on short notice, but she is in constant contact with me. When she comes to visit, I'd like for you to meet her," Lily said with a smile. "That will feel incredibly special."

"You bet. Oh, I just wanted to mention, and hope you don't feel that I'm overstepping my bounds, that I made a reservation at a restaurant close to Fair Gardens for after the cemetery. We'll need to eat something before heading home. This restaurant, named Josie and Her Sisters, has a separate dining area for fifteen to twenty people. Not sure who will be attending the funeral, but I can give them an exact number tomorrow."

"That sounds good to me. I'm grateful that you handled that. I would leave it for twenty people because Dad had some business partners, as well as a few close friends, who he has spoken about and may want to join us. Is that okay?"

"Of course, it's okay. I'll confirm with the restaurant tomorrow."

Lily reclined the passenger seat and catnapped for the half hour until we reached Fairleigh.

CHAPTER 22

The Casket

We arrived a few minutes early to Fairleigh Funeral Home and I pulled into a visitor's spot. It was a shame to have to wake Lily. Leaning back on the headrest, I ruminate about the thoughtful gifts I bought for Teddy over the years to commemorate every special occasion. Today is earmarked for Teddy's final gift selection in a gruesome sort of way. It amazes me to think about the small amount of effort it would have taken for Teddy to please me and show respect for my good nature.

Teddy was incapable of walking in my shoes when all I wanted to do was walk on clouds. Time after time his rain filled the clouds to piss on my parade. My mind was mystified by his fluffy verbiage, telling me I was something special while his steely knife punctured my dreams. I always remained hopeful, though, with each scar that healed, and I continued to try to cut and paste him where I wanted him to be. The Blue Room became my obsession to emotionally connect to his world outside of our home. The Blue Room held great significance, but I could never get past the entrance. And while some sit with their backs to the door for fear that opportunity will open it, I encouraged it. I was ready to walk into a deeper phase of our relationship.

The Blue Room no longer exists for me now. Teddy's body will be stuffed into an 84-inch-by-28-inch-by-23 inch room-for-one to slowly disintegrate, while I stand in front of his claustrophobic chamber with Lily to meet the people I was never introduced to. We will finally gather, but to pass around tissues and not cocktails.

Lily began to stir and opened her eyes. It took her a minute or two to get her bearings, but I didn't rush her. She lifted her cup, took a few sips of the cold coffee, and placed it back in the holder.

"I'm ready, Seppie, let's go inside."

We walked arm in arm to the entrance. Etched on the glass door a quote, "The Purpose of Life is a Life Filled with Purpose," caught my eye. Lily pulled open the door and once inside there was a comforting aroma of apples and cinnamon burning from a candle in the hallway. Farther down the hallway to the right, a wooden shingle read Consulting Office, and as we approached the office a bald gentleman stepped out and introduced himself.

"Good morning. You must be Lily Zezza and..."

"Yes, good morning. This is September, a very close friend."

"Well hello, September," he said, extending his hand. "My name is Charles Dolly, but please call me Charlie. I'm the funeral director. Why don't both of you come into the office and I promise to help you make the decisions as stress-free as possible. Can I offer you coffee or bottled water?"

"No thank you for me," I said and glanced over at Lily. "Lily, would you like something?"

"Oh no, thank you, nothing for me. I'd just like to move through the process quickly. This is very difficult."

"Lily, I certainly understand that and we can begin right away. When you and I spoke on the telephone yesterday we covered a great deal of information and it has all been record-ed into our system. Did you bring your dad's death certificate and deed to the cemetery property?"

"Oh no. I apologize. I'm planning to go to the house tomor-row. All of the documents should be in the safe and I can bring it to you tomorrow, or to the funeral home early Thursday morning before the service begins."

"Very well, then. I know you are contending with a lot. You can bring me the documents by the latest Thursday morning, but preferably tomorrow as you'll be very preoccupied the day of. In the meantime, let me take the two of you downstairs to our showroom. There are several caskets below the $3,000 range, as we discussed. Please follow me."

Lily and I stood up and followed Mr. Dolly down the hall-way and turned left to an elevator.

"How are you doing, honey?" I asked Lily with a reassuring arm around her shoulder.

"Holding up, Seppie, holding up. Please take the lead on choosing the casket, though."

The elevator rattled and the ride down to the bottom floor gave me the chills, as I anticipated entering a dungeon. A loud metallic clanking noise warned us that the elevator would be coming to a stop.

"Watch your step, ladies. There's a small step up out of the elevator."

Lily grabbed my upper arm tightly and we exited together, following Mr. Dolly. He led us into a well-lit showroom. I'm remembering Bart, one of my junior high school friends whose uncle owned a funeral home and the family lived on one of the floors. When we were kids, Bart mentioned that on several occasions when he visited his cousin they would go into the showroom and play hide-and-seek in the caskets. He joked about lying down in one of the caskets as though he were dead, just for the experience, and would ask his cousin to close it. He spooked the shit out of me as he told his story with a twisted grin. Unfucking real. Who can make this up?

Good Time Charlie here knows his craft well and several times was working his persuasiveness on the caskets with a price tag over $3,000. After a short, awkward stroll around the showroom there was a particular casket with a $2,650 price tag that grabbed my attention.

I perversely said to myself, "Sold, to the scorned woman in black; a well-constructed gasketed casket complete with an adjustable bedding system and a matching pillow and throw to make the bastard more comfortable."

"Lily, Mr. Dolly," I called out. "I think I found the casket that seems just right. Shall I show both of you?"

Mr. Dolly came over to the casket and checked the price tag.

"Well, then. This is a good choice. Lily, can we get your approval?"

Lily began walking over to the casket and then stopped.

"We'll go with that one," she said from afar. "Can we go back upstairs now?"

Mr. Dolly escorted us back to the elevator and I could hardly wait to get the fuck out of there, just as quickly as Lily, I would imagine. Once we were back in Charlie's office, he ran Lily's credit card through the machine while I picked the casket and lining colors. After another twenty-five minutes of tying up loose ends Charlie escorted us to the Autumn Room, the parlor where the wake and service will take place, which accommodates 125 people. Lily and I stepped into the parlor and her face became ashen.

"Thank you, Mr. Dolly," I said. "We will see you on Thursday. If we have any last-minute questions we will call you."

"Very well, September."

"Thank you," said Lily, as both of us extended our hand to Mr. Dolly.

He walked us to the entrance, opened the door, and then Lily and I vanished into the parking lot.

CHAPTER 23

The Safe

It's Wednesday morning. I step out of the shower, pick up my phone from the sink top, and notice several missed calls and three voice messages from Lily. Immediately I call back without listening to the messages and after the fifth ring, Lily answers.

"Seppie, I can't breathe. Please come to Greenwich," she pleaded through her sobs.

I'm having déjà vu, remembering the night Lily frantically called for her father and me to come home, the night I left the hotel to look for Teddy in the Blue Room. There had been a handful of times when Lily was in a panic and I had to rush to her. Once Teddy was remiss in picking her up from school after an elementary school ice cream social and she was the last student standing in the school's lobby. It's natural that Lily's anxiety was heightened, fearing that her only remaining parent would abandon her. I am sure that in her head she was running through the worst-case scenarios. I'd tried to explain to Teddy why those episodes occur, but he'd snap at me without forethought and his retort was always condescending, telling me I should stop playing psychiatrist.

"Pea," I said just above a whisper. "Calm, calm. I will come over to you. What happened? Why are you having trouble breathing? Were you lifting something too heavy?"

"Seppie, oh my God, oh my God. I know you don't want to come here, but I'm begging you! What I've found is unspeakable," she shrieked.

"Is Adam with you?" I asked, trying to keep my tone even and soft.

"No, Seppie, Adam isn't here. I'm alone. I need you to come to Greenwich, please. I would never ask you to do this against your better judgment, but I can't, I can't, I just can't..." she said out of breath. Her words were strained and her breathing labored.

"Okay, I'll get dressed quickly and call down to the garage for my car. I'll get to Greenwich as soon as I can. You need to breathe. Can you hang on until I get to you?"

"Yes, yes. I'll leave the back door open. Please hurry and just let yourself in."

My drive to Greenwich was surreal and strangely euphoric. I still remember every route and highway and could drive it with my eyes closed. Traffic is light. Lily's call to me in a frenetic state assures me that there must be a damn good reason that she's upset. My radio is tuned to country music to ease my mind. John Denver's "Take Me Home, Country Roads" is playing and I'm thinking about Jack. Love my boy to the moon and back, and I wish he were in the car holding the top of my hand to his cheek. He has this natural composure and is a calming influence.

The temperature gauge on the dashboard reads fourteen degrees and it's shocking that we didn't have another snowfall from a week ago. Pulling a sharp right off the exit I'm not too far from Teddy's house. Passing all the familiar streets, I turn right onto Crest Drive and then another right onto Lark Lane. Heading down Lark for three blocks Sparrow Lane is fast approaching, and as I turn left onto Sparrow a deep chill grips my body despite the heat in my car. I slowed to five miles per hour, passing their neighbors' pretentious homes. 255 Sparrow, 253 Sparrow, 251 Sparrow, absorbing all the feelings of what once was as I drifted into the driveway of 249 Sparrow Lane.

To the left of the driveway their snow-covered lawn brought back the memory of sitting in the wet snow to pull on my boots, leaving that life to start another.

My breathing is shallow and I let out a moan. "You've got this!"

Grabbing my purse, I stepped out of the car and made my way down the small path leading to the back of the house. The swing set in the backyard had fallen over and is half buried in the snow. Teddy and I would spend hours in that swing, just talking, as he swayed me to believe there was no man better for me than him. The expensive outdoor furniture that we bought together was absent from the yard, no doubt on consignment. Already chilled to the bone I prayed that Lily had cranked up the heat in the house.

My thumb presses the little button on the handle of the glass door to pull it open, then I carefully push open the wooden house door. A soiled bath towel greeted me and I wiped my feet before entering the kitchen. The dim light under the range was turned on and I traveled backward in time.

"Lily. Lily, honey, where are you?"

No answer. My feet padded lightly from room to room and Lily had left the dimmers on in both the den and the living room. All the rooms were barren with the exception of a few extension cords and power strips that have collected a substantial amount of dust.

"Lily, honey, where are you?"

No answer.

My hand caressed the warmth of the banister as I climbed the staircase and I reminisced about the evenings when I'd lock up the house with excited anticipation of curling up under Teddy's arm for the night.

Our bedroom was just to the left at the top of the stairs.

"Lily?"

I turned the doorknob to our bedroom and stepped inside, my eyes scanning every corner of the room. The large closet doors where our clothes once hung together were flung open and bunches of mismatched hangers replaced my beautiful dresses and Teddy's expensive suits. The closed draperies hang with sadness, keep the haunting memories in semi darkness and I'm frozen in time.

Separating the curtains to shed some light on a room that was once filled with passion, a Lancôme mascara and three pennies stared up at me from the dirty windowsill. The mascara wasn't mine, and the three pennies were for my thoughts. My thoughts?

I walked out of the bedroom and peeked into Lily's bedroom. No Lily, so I made my way back down the stairs. This time the banister lacked warmth. Once at the foot of the stairs I looked back up and realized how my world had been turned upside down in an instant.

"Lily, I can't find you," I shouted. "Where are you?"

The basement was door ajar.

"Lily. Lily, it's Seppie. Are you down there?"

Descending the stairs, I heard a stirring and scurried down the remainder of the steps to locate her.

"Seppie, I'm here."

I followed her voice around the corner by the washer and dryer, close to the crawl space, and found Lily sitting on the cold floor with a paper in her hand.

She struggled to speak through her tears.

"Dad kept his safe down here by the entrance to the crawl space. I came to remove the documents that Mr. Dolly requested and to empty whatever else remains. Dad always reminded me that the combination is written in reverse on the back of the safe. Well, I shone the flashlight from my phone to read the combination and my hand touched an envelope taped underneath the safe."

"An envelope?" I questioned.

"It's from my mother, Seppie," she whispered, as she handed it to me. "Read it."

I took the envelope from Lily's hand and my body went numb.

CHAPTER 24

Letter to Lily

The basement was frigid and even colder when I sat down next to Lily on the concrete slab. Lily looked pale and spent, and whatever is written in this letter punctured a deep hole in her soul leaving me with a deflated, empty sack. For the first time I noticed that Lily's little girl features escaped her, now a young woman whose childhood was compromised by the death of her mother. I've reconciled Teddy's mess as much as humanly possible and just when I thought I had nothing left in me, Lily rested her head on my shoulder and I somehow found the strength to endure her trauma. That's what a mother does. Carefully unfolding the letter, I began reading Tessa's words.

My Lily,
If you are reading this letter please know that your mommy traveled to a very peaceful place. I've left our world be-

cause of the deep love that I have for you. There's so much to share and I hope you are old enough to understand why I'm not with you and Daddy. My life hasn't been easy and from the moment that you were a tiny seed growing in my belly, I've always wanted you to have a better life.

Giovanni and Angelina Ricci, my parents, your nonni, raised me in a poor Italian town called Villacidro. My precious girl, they would have adored you! They became penniless shortly after I was born and could barely survive, no less having a child to care for. Despite living far below the poverty level their fairy-tale stories about a princess always opened the beginning of my day with bright hope. I was their princess, without the crown or castle.

An older, somewhat peculiar man named Piero was kind enough to give us food and shelter in exchange for my father working tirelessly in his fields while my mother performed all other duties in his small house. He was a very strict man and often mean-spirited to my parents but treated your mommy extra special. We lived with him for a lot of years until both my parents became ill and passed away. No longer a little girl and in my early teens, I was able to carry out some of the chores, which I learned from watching and helping my mother. Your mommy still needed to survive.

Piero's house was always spotless and my unskilled mother knew the basics of how to prepare food. Everything tasted so delicious. I was heartbroken when Piero would throw the food in the trash, call her a peasant, and tell us to not eat the meal. Hours later I would sift through his trash, remove the food that still looked edible, and secretly brought it to my parents' room. I cannot remember a moment when I wasn't hurting and broken, and when they died I wanted to join *them. Lily, you would have loved your nonni.*

Having nowhere else to live and fearing the streets I stayed with Piero. As I became a young woman Piero would often make me feel very uncomfortable and not allow me privacy in his home. Often I would catch him watching me when I was showering or changing my clothes, and when I closed the door he strictly enforced his rules that all doors in the house remain open at all times. When he realized I was showering in the middle of the night when he was asleep, he turned off the water before he went to bed.

Living with Piero became a nightmare, and when he commanded me to sleep in his bed, I packed the few things that I had and left his house to survive on my own. I thanked the dear Lord that your nonna and nonno were no longer alive to witness Piero's disrespect.

After only a few days of begging for food I went back to Piero, but by that time he had another young girl living in his home and turned me away. Hungry and with no place to go, I survived by performing unrespectable deeds in the eyes of the law and God. The only way I could honor my parents' good name was to survive. Lily, I was an unfortunate girl who didn't choose my past and loved my parents so very much. Hunger got the better of me and no one should have to scour the streets for crumbs.

One afternoon, I remember sitting homeless by the side of a building in a less impoverished area. Three teenage boys passing by stopped to gape at me. One of the boys ate his sandwich as I watched, and I tried to imagine its taste and what it might feel like going into my distended belly. Saving just the crust he spat on the remains then dropped it in my lap. The boys laughed and walked away, likely satisfied that they had their amusement for the day.

I tried to keep myself asleep, mostly to avoid the hunger pangs, and if I got lucky then my dreams would provide me with food. It was much better to live in my dreams.

The day arrived when I was certain that death wasn't far behind. I needed nourishment and if my last ounce of energy wasn't used for survival then the sidewalk would claim my nameless body, dispose of the rags around me, and my soul would drift away with hopes to find my parents. I refused to succumb to life's unfortunate circumstances and all that my family had worked for.

The trash cans became a haven for lost dreams and finding a wrinkled dress beneath a pile of discarded household items was my needle in the haystack. I washed in a gas station bathroom, put on the dress, pinched my cheeks hard for some color, and hoped that any man would pay me for a quick moment of pleasure. I'd sometimes peek into Piero's bedroom when my father was working in the fields and watch him direct my mother on how to pleasure him. I'm doubtful that my father knew about this.

Beautiful like my mother, regardless of what I was wearing and how I smelled, I had some faith that I could attract men. If I weren't taken advantage of, which often I was, and paid for my services, I'd buy a cheap dress and a lip gloss to keep myself marketable. The remainder of my money was used for food.

The streets were harsh and aged me quickly. An abandoned car in a side alley became my shelter until I was pulled from it, half-asleep, early one morning. Lily, my Lily, in order to live I gave away my body, but never my soul or my heart. The two were never connected because I would close my eyes and think about food. After being arrested for sell-ing my body to the devil, Lucia Zezza, my guardian angel took me into her home and cared for me. Lucia was my holy savior, a spinster with no children of her own who knew of my parents.

As my story continues, I met your father, Lucia's great-nephew, when he was visiting her. You must know that at the time I met your father I looked different than when I was found on the streets. Lucia cared for me and insisted that I live with her. She was lonely and valued my company, and in turn I was grateful because she became my only family.

Shortly thereafter, Lucia and I moved to Agerola and started anew. Guilia, who became Lucia's closest friend and owned a small clothing shop, encouraged me to work. Guilia taught me how to greet customers and sell clothes. Before long, she was able to take a day off from work while I man-aged her store. While Lucia argued that she didn't want any of my earned salary, I took pride in giving something back to the woman who saved my life, though she argued with me about doing so.

When your father first saw me, he was captivated by my overwhelming physical beauty, which of course I didn't see in myself. My inner beauty was so simplistic because I was alive with food on a table and a place to sleep. Lucia has al-ways been the true beauty, but I seemed to have charmed your daddy, a successful and handsome lawyer. He swept me off my feet and asked me to travel back to the States with him to get married. Feeling guilty about leaving Lucia, she selflessly gave us her blessing and so our story with you, Lily, begins.

Understand that I didn't know your father well when we

married because everything happened quickly. Lucia and I never spoke of my arrest and how I came to live with her. Lucia passed me off as Guilia's relative who needed a room to rent and there was no need to elaborate. I was respectable and worked hard to obliterate the girl who was found selling herself on the streets.

Years later your father learned of my arrest and let me know he was disgusted, calling me dirty and unworthy. Sharing my heart-wrenching past didn't seem to matter and he angrily contacted Lucia demanding that she never speak of my past, angry with both of us for not disclosing the truth. By that time, I was pregnant with you and often wondered if that was the only reason he stayed with me. I am continually reminded of the lofty lifestyle he has provided, but I believe he married me for selfish reasons. A beautiful wife by his side would complete him and then he demanded that I attend college to round out his résumé. What man of his caliber would have an uneducated street girl for a wife? My life with him over the years has been hell and I tried so hard to make him happy.

"An Italian woman who cannot cook," he would say. "What a joke."

In his cruel moments he would threaten to leave me, gain sole custody of you, and expose my past. It is important that you know the truth from me and I hope that you become a woman of substance and kindness; traits passed down from mother to daughter, my love.

About a year ago your father took me to his firm's holiday event in Manhattan. The beautiful Blue Room is a private room in an upscale restaurant. As you can imagine, he dressed me up as his perfect doll, but deep down inside it was all about the "show." No sooner did he and I walk in together, a stunning older woman approached us and I extended my hand and introduced myself as his wife.

Infuriated, she looked at your father and said, "You're married, you bastard? After all this time I find this out?"

I was devastated and your dad can talk his way out of a paper bag. He is not an honorable man and, Lily, for your sake, I tried my hardest to forgive him, but I've given up my self-respect. If I leave him he will be sure I no longer have you. With all that I have suffered as a child and a young girl, I cannot suffer as an adult. I honestly don't know what is worse, being hungry for food or hungry for self-respect. Lily, Daddy will always cherish you in a way he can never cherish me so I'm certain you will be more than okay.

Tonight at The Beaumont Hotel, Mommy will be at peace. Your father will find me tranquil when he returns from the Blue Room, as I do not plan to go there again. Tonight, there will be no struggle or internal agony, only rainbows and waterfalls. In a luxurious bathtub in a candlelit bathroom, I will swallow a magic pill that will take me to a mystical place to dream. Dream about you and your Great-Aunt Lucia, my lovely gems. Some of Mommy's most peaceful moments had to be in my dreams and we will always be in each other's. I'll reunite with your nonna and nonno on the other side of the rainbow and bring them your picture. If I could live my life over again, I would live it the same way if it meant giving life to you, Lily Zezza, and I will go to sleep with that thought.

Your Mommy

CHAPTER 25

Letter to Lily, The Aftermath

Very carefully, I folded the letter and placed it back in its envelope. The faded blue ink and the fragility of the yellow lined paper was analogous to Tessa's delicate bones lying deep within the earth. How did Teddy handle her suicide? Was he angry that she had ultimate control over her life? Was he crippled by remorse for misperceiving her suffering as he tested her sanity with his senseless infliction of mental strain? Did he visit the suite at The Beaumont every winter to pay homage to the woman he destroyed? His relentless pounding on her ego pummeled her into the ground. How ironic that the walls of her casket protect her from him, in the space where he put her. Tessa found a permanent solution to Teddy's destruction. Can the walls around her safeguard her from the poison that will seep from his casket that lies next to hers? Tessa has earned her passage to eternal peace and if God is righteous, then no angel will collect his soul.

My head hangs low and I struggle to find words that can bring comfort to Lily.

"Lily, your mother was a beautiful and graceful bird; and you, the fortunate girl to have had her in your life although briefly. Let's close our eyes and have a moment of peace. Breathe with me, Lily. Take a deep breath in and then let it out. Imagine the love she carried for you that filled her entire being, as you were her purpose"—(remembering the quote on the funeral home's door)—"She discovered her peace when the angels called for her and it was then that she found her wings to fly away."

I held the letter close to my chest and raised my eyes to the ceiling.

"Our Tessa," I began, "your life will always be remembered as purposeful, appreciated, respected, and celebrated every day in Lily's heart. I promise to honor you by completing the mother/daughter circle in your absence and make us both proud. Rest well."

Lily, her face streaked with blotches of gray from the mixture of tears and mascara, pulled herself up from the concrete floor and knelt in front of the safe. As she twirled the dial to unlatch the combination, I wondered what secrets Teddy left behind in that large, dark crypt.

"Lily, honey," I said in a low voice. "Would you like me to wait for you upstairs? I want to give you privacy."

"Stay with me, Seppie," she said in a whisper.

I watched Lily pull open the door to the safe and she reached inside, returning with a brown accordion folder with thick rubber bands holding it closed, no doubt filled with important documents. Lily placed the folder on the floor next to her and with her left arm did a sweep for anything else that might be inside.

"There's something else in here, Seppie."

She removed a small box and manila envelope taped to it, and placed them on the floor. She also removed what looks like an eight-by-eight-inch square with a pastel cloth fabric wrapped around it. A piece of twine tied them together and was knotted at the top. She closed the safe, spun the dial, and rose to her feet.

Lily looked drained and there were no words of comfort left in my arsenal. I carried the accordion folder under my arm and she walked in front of me holding the two boxes. Once we climbed to the top of the stairs, she stopped in the kitchen and sat on top of the granite counter.

With the boxes cradled in her lap, she picked apart the knotted twine and removed the fabric cover from the square. It was a stained cardboard photo album that read *La Mia Famiglia* and as she turned each delicate page it introduced her to her mother and other family members with their names written on the photographs. In one photo Tessa is wearing the fabric scarf that Lily removed from the album. Lily lifted the fabric to her nose and breathed in deeply as tears flooded her eyes. I watched her open the box that contained a velvet pouch with her mother's wedding band, and Lily tried to fit it on each finger until it slid easily onto her pinky. Inside the manila envelope is Tessa's original death certificate.

She and I placed the contents of the safe into a shopping bag that was wedged between the refrigerator and a cabinet, and we made our way to the back door.

"Here are the house keys, Seppie."

She handed me the keys and walked out into the cold air. I closed the lights in the kitchen, darkening the house on anything else that could further haunt us.

Everything came together in Teddy's death. Everything now makes sense. I pushed open the back door and the backyard's motion light illuminated the path. Ready to take my first step outside, a dead bird appeared next to my foot—an omen, perhaps? I reached into my coat pocket and used a postcard to gently scoop up its fragile shell from the snow and placed it inside the house for warmth.

You are safe, Tessa,

The car ride back to the city was quiet as there was too much to absorb. I was concerned with how Lily would process today because I, myself, am still baffled how a man of Teddy's stature could blatantly misrepresent so many areas of his life, and why? Thinking about the men who I've met, Teddy was the sickest kitten in the litter.

"Animal, animal!" Lily shouted out from her pain.

The volume of her voice scared the crap out of me.

"What am I supposed to do with this? I'm burying my father tomorrow, feeling sad for him, and now this? My mother had to kill herself to have dignity and it's because of him that I have no mother. How will I ever come to terms with this? I'm confused! And oh, the fucking Blue Room. My mother walked into that room with dignity, and he and his mistress grabbed it from her like a worthless possession. For all of her short life she was robbed of the simplest things. And Seppie, you wanted Dad to escort you into that room, thinking it held so much meaning. It's disturbing to think about that room as a haunted playground, or clandestine meeting place, or who knows what?"

As Lily's breath slowed to a normal pace, she put her head back and said, "Seppie, please don't speak of what we discovered today to anyone. I want to bury all of it with him tomorrow and allow my mother dignity in her death."

I reached over with my right hand and touched her cheek, tenderly reassuring her that her wish would be honored. I now understand the significance of the Blue Room, for me, and how it represented a rite of passage into an illusionary life. Now you see it, now you don't. Men like Teddy can easily crush another person's sense of self because they are masters of their craft—sociopathic and narcissistic. The combination is deadly, as is their art of control and manipulation. Challenge them and let them know you've figured them out, and they'll cut you loose and find their daily supply of attention and adoration from another unsuspecting bleeding heart.

Tessa's tears filled the tub that she drowned herself in, as Teddy submerged himself in his lies and deception. The gravity of what has happened is heartbreaking.

The remainder of our drive was quiet and when we arrived at Lily's apartment, she gathered her belongings, stepped out of the car, and walked around to the driver's side. I rolled down my window.

"Love you so much, Seppie," she said, and kissed me on the cheek. "I'll see all of you in the morning. Please remember that I made arrangements for a limo to pick up the family and stay with us throughout the day."

"Yes, of course, I remember and thank you. I will call Sadie and Jack to let them know, too."

As I drove away, I knew that both of us needed time to unpack our day and, without doubt, she will call if she needs to talk. Tonight will be a restless one with little repose. As much as I want to share the events of the day with Wes, it's vital that I honor Lily's wishes. If at any point in her life she wants to share this, it will be her decision to do so.

I reached my apartment just past noon and needed a shower. After shedding my clothes and jumping in the shower, I sat down in the tub and allowed the steady stream of hot water to soothe me. I cried for Lily and her pain.

"Dear God, grant me the strength to help both of us through tomorrow."

CHAPTER 26

The Funeral

There is very little conversation in our apartment this morning, as Wes and I gather our individual thoughts for the day ahead. My clothes are laid out for the funeral. I decided on a long black sweater dress and a pair of short suede boots with a moderate heel. The limo will begin collecting us at nine thirty in the morning to arrive at the funeral home by eleven. The mourners should begin arriving by noon for the twelve thirty service. I'm wondering if Lily plans to deliver a eulogy and am curious what she will say. I trust that whatever she decides will be the right decision.

Wes whipped up one of his specialty omelets, but I am too queasy to eat.

"September, you need to sit for five minutes to eat something before we leave the apartment. You've been running on empty and I don't want you getting sick. Just a few bites will make me happy."

"I know. You're right," I conceded. "It's just that I have a knot in my stomach. Today will be emotionally draining for all of us and I'm most concerned about Lily. She'll need a lot of support, and I'm unsure she'll be able to hold it together."

I stood in front of the bathroom mirror in my bra and panties carefully brushing my eyelashes with mascara. Wes snuck up behind, placing his hands gently on my hips.

"I love the hell out of you, Seppie, and more so because you selflessly do so much for others."

He reached in close and nuzzled his face in my neck to give me a kiss.

"And I am the luckiest woman to have you?" Turning around to give him a hug.

"Indeed, the luckiest woman!" he boasted.

My phone buzzed.

Sadie texted me to confirm that they are on schedule for the pickup, and in turn I placed a quick call to Lily. On the third ring, Adam answered.

"Good morning, Seppie. How are you doing this morning? Thank you for meeting Lily at the house yesterday and driving her home. She appreciated having you there."

"Of course, no worries at all, anything to help. How is she feeling this morning?"

"Lily is okay, seems to be fine. Last night she had a tough time falling asleep, but it's to be expected. She crawled into bed pretty late. She was reviewing the paperwork to prepare for today."

"Sounds good. Just tell her that I called and all of us are on schedule for our pickup. I'll see both of you soon."

My assumption is that she didn't mention anything to Adam about the full contents of the safe. I believe he would have told me.

At ten o'clock the limo picked up Wes and me, and I was glad to find Elle secure in her car seat. Wes held my purse while I climbed in next to Jack, and then he settled into the seat next to me. All of us sat bundled up with our coats and I reached across to extend my hand to Lily. She squeezed mine tightly and gave me a faint smile.

Elle was fussing, but the Cheerios seemed to calm her. Sadie dressed Elle in a black coat and white fur hat, not for the occasion, but because Sadie loves black on a baby. She says it looks chic and makes a fashion statement. Elle's closet is filled with black clothing, but the colorful accessories in her little wardrobe tone it down to appear less morbid. It's difficult to find baby clothing in black so Sadie shops online, mostly Baby Gucci, and pays a handsome price for one-of-a-kind designer pieces. Elle's coat is Yves Saint Laurent. That's Sadie for you!

We arrived a few minutes after eleven. All of us poured out of the limo and made our way to the entrance. Mr. Dolly and another gentleman were there to receive us.

"Good morning, everyone. Good morning, Lily. This is Joseph and he will escort everyone to the coat rack and open up the parlor. Lily, can you follow me to the office to review a few things before the service? I want to briefly discuss the interment, as well."

"Of course," Lily said as she looked over at me. "Seppie, I'll be there soon."

We were escorted to the coat rack and then to the Autumn Room where we immediately smelled the incense. The room was quite large with plenty of seating, but appeared barren. From my experience, the parlor is typically embellished with lots of flowers on stands sent by friends and family. From afar I could see that the casket was open and it sent a shiver down my spine. Behind the casket was only one stand with white roses adorning the sign of a cross. A long table off to the side held a small bouquet in a vase and what looks like a few framed pictures.

All of us took seats in the back and waited for Lily to return. Sadie put Elle on my lap and when she began to squirm, I took out her favorite miniature picture book with the different dogs. Some of the pooches have fur glued to them and all she wants to do is pull the fur off the dogs! Now here's a girl who likely will shave often, I laugh to myself. My granddaughter is a soothing distraction.

After fifteen minutes or so, a tap on my shoulder interrupted my concentration.

"Seppie, please."

Lily held out her hand requisitioning me to accompany her to the front of the parlor.

I shuffled Elle back to Sadie's lap and took a deep breath, my nerve endings tingling.

Lily held my hand tightly and we walked together at a snail's pace.

As we approached the front, Lily dropped my hand and walked ahead to genuflect in front of the casket, cupping her face in her hands. I silently prayed that she found her fortitude as I stood at a comfortable distance not wanting to invade her space.

When Lily stood up, she looked into the casket and stretched her arm back for me to stand by her. I gripped her ice-cold hand and she pulled me closer.

He is an unrecognizable Teodoro Zezza.

Intently, I stared at his eyes and had this urge to pull out the small spiked cups inserted under his eyelids that are keeping them closed, preventing them from caving in. Yes, Teddy, open your eyes and see me! Beautiful September, who rose above the demon. You haven't been around for a while. I did some housekeeping, disposed of the shattered memories and my once crushed spirit, and tossed it with the dirty mess you left behind.

Oh, I must say that these morticians are so incredibly skilled at preparing our loved ones, stuffing the nose and throat with cotton before stitching the jawbone and nasal cavity shut to prevent any of your venom from leaking out. Like anything else, and as you are well aware, it's all about the presentation. Teddy, you are certainly stuffed like a Thanksgiving turkey and there will be no last words from you.

Out of respect for the Christian faith, I lowered myself onto the kneeler to say a prayer. So many thoughts rolled around in my head. At one point my thoughts seemed so sacrilegious that I considered standing up. My prayer? Well, my prayer is for God to keep Tessa protected, and may the good earth remain uncontaminated from Teddy's new home.

I rose to my feet, and Lily was already in the back of the parlor with the family. I stopped for a moment to look at the pictures on the table. There were only a few. Three of the pictures were of Teddy as a young man and one was his baby picture. The largest framed picture was Tessa and Teddy holding Lily as a baby, which I'm certain brought Lily some consolation knowing she had two parents with her somewhere in time. There was another small picture of Teddy, Lily, and me that was taken when she was a little girl and I hoped that Wes wouldn't notice it, although it was a part of my past. It's heartwarming to know that Lily accepts me as her parent, too.

A few people trickled in and Lily motioned me to stand in the front with her and Adam. When I looked back at Wes he nodded and his approval was a welcome comfort.

Four guests signed the book as Lily and I received them. Three were neighbors and one was a former secretary at Pucchi, Pucchi, and Zezza. I awaited the arrival of dozens of people who knew Teddy and wondered if Naomi knew of his passing.

Half an hour later two handsomely suited gentlemen entered, signed the book, and introduced themselves.

"Our deepest sympathy. I'm Salvatore Pucchi and this is my brother Matteo. We were Teddy's partners in the firm."

Both gave Lily a hug, then shook Adam's and my hand. Not asking my relationship, they probably assume I am Teddy's sister or some distant relative.

Few guests walked up to the casket, genuflected to pray, looked at the pictures, and exited.

At about twelve thirty, Lily delivered her father's eulogy, simple, sweet, and heartfelt. Partly out of obligation and partly because I believe she wants to think the best of him in these closing hours.

She delivered the eulogy with no one there but our family.

When the service concluded instructions were given for the procession to Fair Gardens Cemetery. There would be no cars following the hearse with the exception of our limo. Lily collected the photos, the sign-in book, and the two hundred memorial cards that would end up in the trash. I felt her devastation, as the room remained almost as empty as when we arrived. She and the family left the parlor to collect their coats.

When the room emptied, I walked back to the casket.

"Now it's just the two of us, Teddy," I said, looking down at him in a twisted sort of way.

With deep concentration I stared at him and searched for a feeling, but I felt nothing. There were no butterflies in my stomach when I thought about our passion. All of his money couldn't buy enough people to attend his funeral or repair the damage he imposed on his wife and daughter. My long-standing fantasy of walking into the Blue Room on his arm frightens me now.

"You are handsomely clothed in lies and a bow tie," I chuckled.

I am so proud of myself. I really have moved on. My searching brought me to a stronger place than when I started.

I blinked my eyes several times, looked away from the casket and then looked back. Teddy's peanut-size head and emaciated body is shrouded in a powder blue satin-lined casket with matching blue bedding. I tried hard to imagine the blue satin as bedsheets and how I would feel rolling around in them with him. Still nothing.

"Blue, blue, blue; blue is everywhere, Teddy Zezza," I said firmly.

"I'm wondering if Lily even noticed that the casket has a cobalt blue finish? Yes indeed, with silver highlights. After all, Teddy, I was given the privilege to select your casket, and in my warped mind it gives me profound pleasure to know you will decompose in your very own tiny blue room."

I sensed a stirring behind me and when I turned, I was startled to see a young girl standing a foot behind me. She appeared out of nowhere.

"Excuse me, I don't mean to intrude, but how do you know Miss Betty?" the girl asked.

"Who is Miss Betty and you are?"

"I'm Jess. I came to pay respects to Miss Betty."

"This is not Miss Betty, and this is the Autumn Room," I confirmed.

"I am so, so sorry. I wandered into the wrong parlor," she apologized as she peeked into the casket.

"That's quite all right, no worries."

"Can I ask you a question? I know I should mind my own business."

"Yes, of course," curious about what she might want to know.

"I stood back and watched you, not knowing it wasn't Miss Betty and not knowing who you are. Your expressions toward the person you are paying respect to seem angry. I mean I'm upset about being here, too."

"You're right about that, and your name again?"

"Jess, my name is Jess."

"Well, Jess, there is something to be said about having the last word. The person lying in this casket is in a better place. A better place for all of us."

"Hmm, I'm sorry that your loved one suffered."

"Well, Jess, you might be the only one to feel sorry for this carcass," I said with certainty and a smile.

"It's hard to imagine that this person created so many bad feelings for you to feel no pity."

Jess looked shocked and unsettled by my response.

"Well, dear, it's a very long story with events that nearly destroyed me. A story I'll never rehash or want to remember once I leave here."

"I'd best be on my way to find Miss Betty. For whatever it might be worth, I'm still sorry for your loss."

I nodded.

As Jess was leaving the parlor, Mr. Dolly walked back inside. He approached me by the casket, businesslike, and I could tell he was ready to move the process along to prepare for the next parade of mourners.

"Excuse me, September. Your family is waiting for you and it's time to close and latch the casket."

I peeked into the casket one last time and smiled, then turned to Mr. Dolly.

"Of course, Charlie. I'm done here."

ACKNOWLEDGEMENTS

First and foremost, I have to thank my parents for encouraging me, at a very young age, to dream big! As my greatest teachers who taught from the heart, your lessons on patience, self-appreciation, and the importance of remaining grounded, gave me wings to fly.

To my children Samantha Rae and Dean Spencer, you are truly the greatest of my accomplishments and my character is best judged by how you have blossomed into strong, wise, and successful adults. I taught you integrity and kindness and now you are guiding that moral compass.

Samantha Rae, your artistic talent, budding since elementary school, has transcended to a career as an award-winning designer. It gives me insurmountable pride that you designed this book cover to capture the true essence of the story. A picture is worth a thousand words!

To Scott, my younger brother and punching bag until

you were old enough to strong-arm me, I love you to pieces! Though still "partners in crime," since childhood, somehow we created balance for each other. Our beautiful families have enriched our journey.

My deep appreciation to Tony Ford, my dear friend and fellow writer, who has spent endless hours listening to my reading each chapter upon its completion. Searching for September has been my labor of love, and your continual love and encouragement has helped me deliver this baby!

Extending extreme gratitude to my close friends, some who served as beta readers, who believed in my storyline with the turn of each page. As women, it is crucial to acknowledge and own our feelings about our relationships, in partnership with discovering our voice. Shared experiences incentivized me to construct the characters in Searching for September. I listened, I heard, and our affirmations reverberate through the life of my characters.

After quite a bit of digging, Cheryl Benton, my publisher, you are the diamond in the rough. Your commitment to reading just three chapters of my book turned into reading it in its entirety, in one sitting. Thank you for finding value in my work as a writer and taking the reins to eagerly promote *Searching for September* to a wide audience.

ABOUT THE AUTHOR

 Robin A. Lieberman is an educator turned novelist. Throughout her career as school counselor, she has nurtured her writing through memoirs and poetry. *In Searching for September*, her debut novel, she called on her own triumph through personal disappointments and unbounded joys which have given her the impetus to share a view of the world through her lens, with creativity and vivid imagination. Ardently putting pen to paper, she invites her audience to join her on this journey through a powerful story line.

A native New Yorker born in Brooklyn, Robin has remained true to her roots by raising her daughter and son in New York with its buzzing, unparalleled energy. She resides in Manhattan and fills her personal life with world travel and quality time with her family and intimate circle of friends.

*****

If you enjoy the book, please leave a review on Amazon or Goodreads.

*****

The story of September and Lily will continue in the sequel which will be published in 2022. For details and updates visit Searchingforseptember.com

CPSIA information can be obtained
at www.ICGtesting.com
Printed in the USA
LVHW092139150621
690345LV00014B/147/J

9 781736 494950